THE FILE ON Fraulein Berg

THE FILE ON Fraulein Berg

JOAN LINGARD

Julia MacRae Books

First published in Great Britain 1980 by
Julia MacRae Books
A division of Franklin Watts
8 Cork Street, London W1X 2HA
Copyright © 1980 Joan Lingard

Lingard, Joan
    The file on Fraulein Berg.
    I. Title
    823'.9'1J   PZ7.L6626

    ISBN 0-86203-000-5

Reproduced from copy supplied
printed and bound in Great Britain
by Billing and Sons Limited
Guildford, London, Oxford, Worcester

For Julia MacRae
in gratitude
for all her help and encouragement
and with much affection

PROLOGUE

We met in London, briefly, our paths crossing for an hour or two, as they had done at intervals over the past twenty years. Once we had been close, 'thick as thieves', as our mothers put it, and had never imagined we could ever stay more than a week apart. That was a long time ago, at school, in Belfast.

Sally laughed about that time now. "What horrors we were! Monsters, in fact." And as if that had triggered her memory, she added, "Oh, by the way, you'll never guess who we met when we were in Vienna!" No, I couldn't begin to guess so I didn't try. "Fraulein Berg!"

"Fraulein Berg?" I had to put my cup to rest in its saucer. The coffee was about to slop. I stared across the table at Sally's smiling face. "I don't believe it."

"True. Cross my heart! Wasn't it extraordinary? She remembered you."

"She did?" There were times when one did not wish to be remembered.

"Us. The three of us. You and Harriet and I."

I was still staring. Sally was still smiling, pleased at my surprise. Where Fraulein Berg was concerned, I could think of no reason to smile.

"Well, she had good reason to remember us, didn't she? I mean, after all, I suppose you could say we did give her rather a hard time."

"We persecuted her," I said very quietly, to myself more than to Sally, for already I was ceasing to see her and instead could visualise the face of a sallow-skinned woman before me. It was the eyes that jumped out of the past so remarkably vividly: they were dark and imploring. And then I realised that Sally had heard what I had said for she had stopped smiling.

Fraulein Berg came to our school in the early days of 1944. They were dark days in Britain; the war had been dragging on for more than three years and showed no sign of being brought speedily or decisively to an end. People were weary of shortages, the blackout, and being separated from their menfolk who were away fighting on the various fronts; they were weary of making do and being told not to grumble. And they were tired of the sound of air raid warnings; at least in London they must have been.

Belfast was quiet. Too quiet, said Sally: like a graveyard at two in the morning. She wouldn't have minded a bit of fire fighting. The Germans seemed to have forgotten about us, as far as air raids were concerned. We had had our share earlier on in the war, when they had been aiming for the shipyards. There were plenty of blitzed squares and jagged-edged buildings to testify to that, as well as boarded-up windows and cracked walls. Our ceilings looked like crazy paving and did till the day we sold the house because my mother couldn't afford to have anything done about them. Sally's father, who could, got a grant to sort his bomb damage. My mother always had plenty to say about Sally's father, although she seemed to like him well enough. "He's all right in his own way," she would say, meaning in spite of all the things about him that she disapproved of. He owned a butcher's shop at the beginning of the war but did so well on the Black Market that by the end of it he owned a chain of shops and toured around them in a long black car to make sure he wasn't being diddled.

There was not too much excitement either from servicemen coming home on leave swathed in bandages with tales of bravado to tell, or people receiving telegrams from the War Office in the middle of the night, for we had no conscription in Northern Ireland. Quite a number of young men and women did volunteer, from both north and south of the border, but we didn't know many of them and those we did never seemed to leave the province. They were neutral over the other side of the border, in Eire, a fact we much resented. Sally's father had a good laugh when the Germans bombed Dublin in mistake for Belfast in May 1941. "Serve the so-and-sos right!" he declared, bringing his chopper down on the board with extra vigour.

And so our interest in the war flared intermittently, as for example when we went to the cinema, were stirred by the newsreels, and saw German planes spiralling earthwards in flames, or when we read spy stories. Spies triggered our imaginations and we longed to be dropped behind enemy lines where we would perform deeds of incredible daring, steal secret messages from under the noses of the S.S., and bring out escaped British airmen.

"Anything would be better than sitting around in this dump," said Sally, whilst we sat waiting for the arrival of the geography teacher who bored the living daylights out of us. She was about ninety-two years old and had been brought out of retirement for the war. Even our mothers were more involved in real wartime life, sitting in their A.R.P. post doing their knitting and drinking tea and recalling the nights of

April 1941 when they hadn't had time to knit and the sirens had wailed and the anti-aircraft guns had chattered from Cave Hill and the bombs came whistling down. (I had slept throughout, to my shame and chagrin, and so could not compete with Harriet's first-hand account.) Sally's and Harriet's fathers were in the Home Guard and they had been out there rescuing people from burning houses and taking the injured to the hospital. After the bombing, Sally's father had tried to make bombs using petrol, to help towards the war effort, and blown the back end of his garage out. My own father was dead, long before the war started.

There was a time when we too had knitted, gloves for airmen whose hands would need to have been distorted to fit them. And we collected money for the Red Cross from time to time. But one thing we were consistent about and were encouraged to be: we hated Germans.

So, when a real live German arrived in our midst to teach us, our interest was aroused and we sat up straight and lifted our heads to take careful note of her.

"This is Fraulein Berg, girls," said the headmistress, who was wrapped in two cardigans and two skirts to ward off the chill of that January day. We could see them all for they overlapped. "We are most fortunate in having been able to procure her services. I am sure you will make her welcome." She fixed us with her ice-blue stare which said more than a string of words could. "Fraulein Berg, this is the Lower Fourth."

The Lower Fourth stared at Fraulein Berg. The room was completely quiet, for once. A red stain was creeping up the German woman's neck to tinge her sallow cheeks with colour. And from out of that face gazed dark eyes which burned with such intensity they made us shift on our hard seats. They were appealing to us, though we did not recognise that then. Or perhaps we did, but were not prepared to respond. We could see at once that she was going to be useless as a teacher, she would not be able to keep control, and we would become uncontrollable. Although we grumbled, we liked best the teachers who could keep order. Weakness is seldom appealing, at least not when you're young. Her Adam's apple jerked up and down. She seemed to wish to speak but no sound emerged from her pale lips. The tip of her tongue moistened them.

"She's got tufts of hair on her chin," said Sally, her breath hot in my ear. She was in the desk behind me. I stuffed my handkerchief half-way into my mouth. I could feel Sally's desk shaking.

"Stand up, Sally MacCabe, and tell us what you have just said to Kathleen Carson."

She couldn't repeat it of course, so made up some lie which was scarcely convincing but had to be accepted by the headmistress who by then had realised it was a question she should not have asked. She was terribly keen on the truth, exhorted us at morning prayers never to lower ourselves to the telling of falsehoods, but she would not have been keen to have her staff insulted.

Her staff. They were a motley looking lot, spinsters all but two, and even one of those was widowed. Men were not thought much of, and if the headmistress could have managed it, she would have had boys outlawed from the country, or at least sent to the front lines whence, with a bit of luck, they might not return. She had told us that if she ever caught us talking to one in the street she would come over and shame us before him. She also felt strongly about wearing gloves and hats in the street. It all seems archaic now: both the rules and the staff. She was unable to pay for too many well-trained teachers. It was a private school and got the rag-bag end of the market, so said Sally. I had got in on a scholarship, otherwise I wouldn't have been there since my mother did not have the money for the fees. She took in sewing for a living, and, as she said, we couldn't live very highly on that.

12

The headmistress gave each of the known troublemakers another quick warning glance, then left Fraulein Berg to our mercies. She could not have got the length of her study before the noise broke out in room ten.

"*Bitte!* Please." Fraulein Berg rapped on her little brown attaché case with raw red knuckles. The gesture was to become exceedingly familiar to us during the months she stayed in our school. She did, in fact, speak quite good English, not that she got the chance to use much of it in that first lesson.

"Stands to reason she would speak good English," said Harriet, as we were walking home. "Well, of course. They always teach their spies to speak English. They wouldn't be much good if they couldn't, would they?"

Yes, it was Harriet who first labelled her a spy: I remember distinctly her cool, clear voice speaking a little derisively as if we should have had enough wit to realise it for ourselves. Oh, not that I want to opt out of responsibility, not at all; I'm just trying to set the record straight, get the facts down as they happened, if that's possible. Retelling the past is always tricky, and no doubt each of the three of us would have a different tale to tell.

We eyed Harriet who was walking fast and looking straight ahead. She was in a hurry, had a ballet lesson at four, and she had longer legs than we did anyway. We quickened our steps. Her long silky blond hair fluttered back in the wind. She was going to be a beauty, said my mother, who made clothes for her. She had a high forehead and fine grey eyes, and she talked with a slightly Anglicised accent. When we fell out with her, which happened from time to time, just as we all fell out with one another in different combinations, Sally would mock her voice and put on the most excruciating Oxford accent, or what we thought was an Oxford accent. We didn't know anyone who had been to Oxford. Nearly all our teachers had been to Queen's University, Belfast, if they had been to any university at all.

"Do you think she was dropped in by a German plane during the night?" Sally giggled and I joined her, caught up in a vision of Fraulein Berg plummetting earthward, clinging to the end of a parachute with one hand and holding her little attaché case in the other.

"Don't be daft." Harriet turned now and waited for us to catch up. "Honestly, Sally!"

"Oh, I know I'm a right eejit." Sally grinned.

"How would she have come in?" I asked.

"She'll have come in over the border of course. Spies slip over all the time. It's dead easy." She spoke impatiently as if again we should have known. We did know there was some trafficking of German agents from Eire into Northern Ireland; every now and then one was caught, or so we heard from Harriet. She had an advantage over us when it came to inside information since her father was a lawyer. From her we heard about criminal goings on that ranged from the activities of the Irish Republican Army to housebreaking. Watch what you say to her, Sally's mother warned us, and I supposed she meant about Mr MacCabe and his meat. We weren't up on too much other crime.

But we were aware that spies were a problem in wartime. And we had seen the posters often enough which said: *Walls have ears. Careless talk costs lives.* That used to worry me. What was careless talk? I couldn't be sure that I was not talking carelessly and was afraid that, without meaning to, I might give away valuable information to an enemy agent.

"But if she was a spy wouldn't she pretend to be English?" I objected.

"How could she? With an accent like that?"

"She could have said she was Dutch," suggested Sally.

"She probably can't speak Dutch." Harriet had an answer to most things.

"She could have learned Dutch," said Sally.

14

"Well, she obviously didn't."

We had a brief pause to nip into a shop for ice cream. I only had a penny ha'penny so Sally lent me the balance to make up threepence. We walked a little more slowly now, licking as we went.

"But wouldn't she have been put in a camp when the war started?" I said.

"She could have come in before the war and got naturalised." We were not sure what naturalised meant but didn't enquire. When I asked my mother later she said it meant taking out British citizenship. Harriet continued, "The Germans were getting ready for years, you know. They had their spies set up all over the place." This did not quite tie up with what she'd just said about Fraulein Berg having been slipped in over the border. We did not protest.

We turned off the main road into the street where I lived. We passed the row of brick back-to-backs, the end one of which had a mural of King William of Orange with his white horse on the gable wall, crossed another street opening and then came to the row of terraced houses where I lived. They were bigger and better than the back-to-backs but we had no garden in front although we did have a small one behind, not that I found that much compensation. I longed for a long front garden, a high wall, tall trees, and a house set back from the street. Outside my door, we stopped for a moment. Sally lived a little further along in a semi-detached house, and Harriet about half a mile beyond that in a Tudor-style detached house. Later, Sally's family were to move into a detached house too, a much bigger and grander one than Harriet's. In those days it all seemed to matter: the size of people's houses, if they had a car and a telephone or not. We didn't even have a telephone. My mother said we had no use for one.

"Come on then, Sally, if you're coming." Harriet was impatient now to be off: ballet was calling. We said our goodbyes and I went inside, automatically calling out to my mother as I opened the door.

"In here."

She was in the front room, our sitting and her sewing room. We had a kitchen at the back, and two bedrooms upstairs. She had a customer who was being fitted for an evening dress. It was Harriet's mother.

"Say hello to Mrs Linton, dear."

Why did she have to tell me what to do when I had been about to do it anyway? I said hello and felt sulky. I slid round the back of a dummy wearing a tweed costume and got to the fire. Oh, the warmth of it! I held out my cold hands to the leaping flames. I felt my body slacken. And how was I? Mrs Linton wanted to know. Fine, I said. And school? Fine too. What was the point of going into any details? I was sure she didn't want to know but she was a very polite, well-mannered woman, as my mother said after each of her visits. She stood, feet slightly apart, head held well up, her body encased in black satin, and my mother knelt on the hearth rug in front of her, with pins in her mouth and an inchtape round her neck. She approved of my mother, so I gathered from Harriet, though not of Sally's. Mrs MacCabe she found common; my mother was a gentle-woman down on her luck.

My mother stood, rubbing her knees to ease them off. She tweaked the dress, nodded. Did Mrs Linton want any decoration?

"Sequins, perhaps? Just a touch round the neckline and waist. What do you say, Kate? Do you think that would look nice?" She smiled. "Are you interested in clothes? Harriet, as you no doubt know, just adores getting dressed up."

Since my mother could not match the statement she said nothing. She asked me to go and put the kettle on and make Mrs Linton a cup of tea.

16

I made the tea, set a tray with a well-worn embroidered cloth and two cups from my mother's fine china tea set. In the cake tin I found some chocolate cake and cut it into three pieces, laying the largest bit aside for myself. I carried in their tea — Mrs Linton was telling my mother about a ball she was going to at Belfast Castle — and then scurried back to the kitchen to guzzle my cake. It was moist and delicious, and had been made from liquid paraffin instead of fat. We were rationed for butter and margarine of course. Of liquid paraffin there seemed to be an infinite supply.

When I heard the front door close behind Mrs Linton I went back to the sitting room. My mother was turning the black satin dress inside out.

"I've just remembered, Kate, I'm out of black thread. Will you go to Mrs McCurdy's for me?"

It was getting dark as I made my way back up the street to the main road where the shops were. The street lights wouldn't come on of course because of the blackout. I couldn't imagine streets at night seeming as bright as day but that was what people said it was like before, and would be again. Though it was taking a long time, sighed my mother; they'd never thought the war would go on this long. They had expected to beat the Gerries by 1940. But no wonder they didn't, I thought, as I dawdled along, kicking a stone part of the way, hopping up and down the side of the kerb, not when the Germans had been so well prepared beforehand. A car tooted at my back and I retreated into the middle of the pavement.

I skirted a couple of kids playing hopscotch and another careering up and down on a bogey cart. I looked covetously at the bogey. I was supposed to be past such things, growing up, getting to be quite a little lady. I hated all the phrases my mother's customers used about me.

The traffic was busy on the main road. People were coming home from work. A trolley bus passed packed with faces. Mr MacCabe waved to me from behind a leg of lamb. At that time he was still working in his shop. He wore a butcher's overall and had his sleeves rolled up to his elbows. He was cleaning up for the end of the day. I waved back, passed the greengrocer's, and turned into Dyson's sweet shop where I had my sweet coupons lodged. I bought my ration in driblets, a pennyworth at a time, to eke it out and prolong the pleasure.

"A pennyworth of liquorice balls, please, Mr Dyson."

He leant on the counter and we had a little chat. He was always ready for a chat since business in a sweet shop in wartime could not be brisk. I told him about Fraulein Berg.

"Gerry eh? Fancy that!" But he didn't seem interested to discuss her any further for he went on to tell me about the old days, his favourite topic, when anyone could buy half a dozen boxes of chocolates and ten pounds of toffees at a go if they felt like it. I used to feel my teeth begin to ache as he described it. Before I left he slipped a chocolate violet into my hand.

I still associate that peculiar perfumed taste with Fraulein Berg for I was still sucking the sweet when I went into Mrs McCurdy's haberdashery and encountered her there.

She was buying a card of pink elastic. The middle of the counter was covered with cards of elastic, of different widths and colours. Flanking them stood boxes upon boxes of buttons and ribbons, ankle socks, babies' mittens, safety pins and needles. Mrs McCurdy's shop was a glorious muddle and sometimes she let me help her on a Saturday. I loved standing behind the counter, rolling ribbons, sorting skeins of embroidery thread of every colour imaginable. It was like being in a brightly coloured treasure trove.

Mrs McCurdy said, "Hello there, Kate," and then resumed talking to her customer in a very loud voice that people often put on for foreigners, seeming to think that loudness will make words easier to understand. As it happened, Fraulein

Berg probably had a better command of the King's English than did Mrs McCurdy.

"I'll take this one, thank you." She rummaged in her purse and laid some money on the counter. She glanced sideways to smile at me. I occupied myself looking at the new range of knitting wool that had just been put on the shelf.

"Kate's mother's the one I was telling you about," said Mrs McCurdy. "The dressmaker."

I felt myself freeze.

"Ah, is that so? I am looking for a dressmaker, Kate. I need some new costumes." I was silent. She hesitated. "I wonder if she would be interested?"

"Oh, I'm sorry," I jumped in quickly, cutting her off. "But she's absolutely up to the eyes at the moment. She couldn't possibly take on another customer."

I sensed that she knew that I lied. She backed away from the counter clutching her thin brown paper parcel to her chest. She looked rejected.

"Thank you, miss," said Mrs McCurdy.

"Good day." Fraulein Berg gave a little half bow and backed out of the shop. A gust of cold air swirled in around my legs. The door jingled shut.

Mrs McCurdy shoved the remaining cards of elastic aside and leant her plump arms on the counter. "Didn't know your mother was that busy? Thought she was always glad of any work she could get. In these days with the coupons and that, it's not easy."

Fraulein Berg hadn't shut the door properly. An extra strong puff of wind blew it open again. I went to shut it and before I did stole a quick glance out into the street. Fraulein Berg was still standing on the pavement only a couple of feet away. She looked kind of lost and forlorn as if she didn't know where to go next. For a moment I almost called out to her, I wanted to, but I hesitated not knowing quite what

19

words to use, and in that moment she moved away. I closed
the door.

By next morning Harriet, naturally, had some information on Fraulein Berg.

"We might have known," said Sally to me in an aside. She herself would not have given the German teacher another thought after we'd parted yesterday: life in the MacCabe household was always too hectic and demanding for outside matters to intrude too much. I had spent the evening trying not to think about Fraulein Berg. I'd immersed myself in a book by L. M. Montgomery, *Emily of Lantern Hill*, set on Prince Edward Island, which was pretty remote in spirit and place from Belfast and thoughts of German spies.

At tea my mother had said she was a bit worried, she didn't have too many orders on her books, and she was wondering if she should advertise in the *Belfast Telegraph*. My guilt had dampened my appetite and I hadn't been able to finish my fried haddock, which led to my mother giving me a lecture on food waste. I was prone to feeling guilty about all sorts of things. Sally, who never seemed to feel guilty about anything, said I should have been born a Catholic, it would have been dead handy to be able to go to confession, to be given five Hail Marys to say as a penance, and then I'd be absolved. She didn't say that to me in her own house, she wouldn't have dared, for her father was a staunch Protestant and a member of the local Orange Lodge. He walked on the twelfth of July, bowler-hatted and sashed, in the parade to celebrate the Battle of the Boyne in 1689. Mention the Pope in his house and he'd choke on his fried steak.

During Prayers Harriet managed to convey to us that she had found something out about our new teacher but she was not going to give it all away at once, and especially with Miss Thistlethwaite for competition. The headmistress was enthusing lyrically on one of her favourite topics: headgear. We must wear hats in the street and we must not wear coloured ribbons with our school uniform except for emerald green which was one of the school colours. The other was grey. We wore grey hats, grey coats, grey tunics. We looked like a flock of grey owls, said Mr MacCabe. Looking back, I only recall the headmistress haranguing us over trifles, never over matters of idealism or the intellect. The only time idealism came to the fore was on Empire day when the Union Jack was placed at the head of the hall and we all had to file past and salute it. Even though I was a Girl Guide for a while, I always felt silly saluting the flag and as my hand came up I was sure to hear Sally's giggle behind me. And then I'd look at Miss Thistlethwaite's face and see that it was serious to a point of being enrapt. She must have been dreaming about the glories of British rule in India and Fiji and the Gilbert and Ellice Islands. It was a great blow to her when India got its independence. A backward step, girls, she said to us in history, the subject which she herself taught. Her father had planted tea in Assam.

Ignoring the shuffle of restless feet and the steadily increasing hack of winter coughs, Miss Thistlethwaite continued on her theme — she had an obsession about the neatness of clothes, she who dressed so untidily herself — and Harriet dropped hints that were intended to tease, and did.

22

We had to wait till we were in the chemistry lab and curling one another's hair with the crucible tongs. Lab was rather a high-sounding name for the scruffy room which had once been a stable and now boasted of a few bits and pieces of the more basic scientific equipment. Science was not strong at our school; it was impossible to take physics to higher level and those who took chemistry did so at their own risk. We most of us gave up after Junior Certificate. The whole school was makeshift, having once been an ordinary dwelling house on which not too much money had been spent for conversion.

Harriet was curling my hair which was thick and heavy and black. It wasn't too keen to curl but Harriet was persistent.

"Come on, Harry," urged Sally, whose hair *I* was curling. Harriet never allowed us to touch hers: she said it was much too fine.

"You know Susan Andrews who lives next door to me?"

Yes, yes! We were impatient. In a minute the chemistry teacher would reach our group to see how we were getting on with the experiment we were supposed to be doing and had nothing to do with the curling of hair. It turned out that Fraulein Berg had taught at Susan Andrews' school, for six months.

"She was dismissed!" said Harriet.

Suddenly I became aware of a strong smell of singeing. It was coming from my head. I yelped, the crucible tongs touched my neck, and I yelped again, more loudly, and so attracted the attention of the teacher who went into a tizzy and flapped her hands and screeched at us. We were impossible. We were unteachable. The rest of the class were now eating their mid-morning snacks and chatting in peace.

The door opened, and in came Miss Thistlethwaite. She was constantly on the rove, like a police constable on the beat. One thing she could not do was carry a gun at her hip as the police did in Ulster, but we felt sure she would have liked to. We were removed to her study where we stood on the half-moon rug as close to the fire as we could get. The heat felt good on the backs of our cold knees. The school was like an ice box in winter, but no matter how desperate the fuel shortage became, the coals never burned low in the headmistress's grate.

She was surprised at us, she said, especially at Harriet, who she had not yet labelled as a troublemaker. She knew her father and two of her aunts. Delightful women. What would her father think? she demanded. What would my mother think? She did not ask what Sally's parents would think.

We apologised, meekly, with eyes cast down at the brown rug which was curly round the edges and worn almost bald in the middle. The headmistress turned back to her desk and began to write sternly on a piece of paper. She was only writing staff notes, said Sally afterwards, who was nearest and had remarkably sharp eyesight. We had to stand mutely, hands behind our backs, resisting the impulse to scratch, until the period bell sounded and gave us our release.

From there we went to Latin which was a class that offered no opportunity for conversation. Miss Bell, head decorated with coiled grey plaits, was a martinet who put up with no disobedience of any kind. Once Sally had tried dropping a pin and we actually heard it fall.

So it was not until the morning interval that we got the rest of Harriet's information. We walked down to the end of the garden and stood beside the wet privet hedge.

We waited.

"She was dismissed for incompetence."

"Oh! Is that all?" We were understandably disappointed, having expected something, if not criminal, then at least more exciting than that. One look at Fraulein Berg and we had known she was incompetent.

"No, that's *not* all." Harriet finished her sandwich and licked her fingers. "She was living in Dublin before that!

24

I told you, didn't I? She got in over the border. It's easy as pie. There's dozens of places you can just walk across, especially after dark."

I thought of Fraulein Berg crossing a field at night, buttoned shoes clogged with mud, attaché case in her right hand.

"Susan says she heard she taught in several different schools in Dublin."

"Dismissed from each one for the same thing, I suppose," I said.

"Probably ran out of schools," said Sally. She had a packet of chocolate biscuits, of all things! She gave us one each. Her family got anything it wanted. Mr MacCabe provided the meat and his wife did the bartering. Whenever there was a tap at the MacCabes' back door you never knew who would come in carrying what. It could be anything from a big wheel of yellow cheese to a couple of cans of petrol.

"Or else it suited her to move around," said Harriet. "That way no one could keep tabs on her. And that is obviously what we've got to do."

"Do what?" asked Sally, spraying me with biscuit crumbs.

"Keep tabs on her."

The bell rang then. We crammed another biscuit into our mouths and ran across the soggy grass to join the back of the queue.

We had Fraulein Berg in the afternoon, though not for German. There weren't enough classes in the school to keep her occupied teaching German so she had to help out with all sorts of other activities, like supervising hockey practice or taking on the classes of absent teachers. She was taking us for sewing that day. It was usually a class that was reasonably peaceful since sewing seems to calm people down. You could sit and work at your own pace, rest a bit now and then and let your thoughts wander. I was not particularly good at it, tending to make my stitches too large and get the material grubby. She soon noticed my lack of skill when she came round to see if we wanted any help.

"I thought you would have been a perfect little needle-woman, Kathleen," she said, bending over me, "since your mother is a dressmaker."

I scowled and blushed. And then I suffered agonies of guilt all over again for here I was feeling ashamed at having it spelled out in public that my mother was a dressmaker. All Harriet's relations did such interesting, elevated things; or else, if they were women, they sat at home and gave tea and bridge parties. Such snobbery was no doubt very un-attractive, but I have to admit that I was party to it, then. I also hated Fraulein Berg for her clumsy remark and she saw that I did, for her face had flushed and she was biting her lip. As well as being incompetent when it came to handling a class, she was socially inept even with her peers. We saw her blush many a time whilst talking to another teacher and then turn away with that characteristic annoyed little frown.

She straightened her back. She smelled of Eau de Cologne. Cologne. A city on the Rhine. No British woman would have worn perfume with a name like that, I felt sure.

I said so, as we came out of school. Now I felt hardened towards her.

"The case looks pretty bad against her," reflected Harriet.

"What did you mean about keeping tabs?" asked Sally. We were going home to Sally's, for tea, a treat we much enjoyed.

"Watch her. Follow her. Trail her. Find out who her contacts are."

"We'll work like detectives," I said.

"Secret service agents," corrected Harriet. "There is a war on, you know, and this is espionage we're dealing with."

Her words thrilled us. We went up the hill in the pouring rain forgetting to put up the hoods on our burberrys so that we arrived at the shops with our heads soaked.

26

"You'll get your death," said the woman in the stationer's. "Look at you, Kate! Your ma wouldn't like to see that. And you hardly out of your bed with bronchitis the whole month of December."

I shook my head and scattered raindrops on her display of writing paper which gave her further cause to moan. Grown-ups always seemed to be moaning about something, I thought.

We made our purchases, a notebook and a short pencil each. Harriet thought a pencil would be easier to handle, much less messy than a fountain pen, in difficult situations.

"Difficult?" asked Sally, as we stood sheltering in the shop porch.

Harriet was vague. "Well, on street corners and places. You might have to hang about in the rain. Ink runs when it gets wet."

We gazed out at the rain which was coming down like a solid curtain and bouncing angrily off the pavement. A shrouded figure, clasping an umbrella, and listing slightly in the wind, went past. It was Fraulein Berg.

"Quick!" cried Harriet. "After her!"

We scuttled along the pavement kicking up water at one another's ankles. In our pockets we clutched our notebooks and pencils. Fraulein Berg did not look back, she was too anxious to get home. We made up on her until we were only about ten yards behind. Visibility was not much more than that.

She halted abruptly and so did we, half tripping over one another. We took a few steps backward and a man behind coming at speed with a thin whippet on a leash cursed us. The whippet would have liked to sniff our legs but was urged on. Our quarry was looking in her purse, holding her umbrella at an awkward angle against her shoulder whilst she did so. She had been looking for her key. We saw her hold it up.

Two more paces, and she stopped at a door and unlocked it. She went inside. The door was between two shops, the ironmonger's and the shoemaker's, and must lead to a flat above one or the other or both.

We went first into the ironmonger's and Sally bought a pennyworth of screws.

"I was just wondering, Mr Boyd," she said, leaning on the counter in the way that Mrs McCurdy and several other shopkeepers did, and which Harriet would never do for she liked to stand straight and tall, "where that door next to you goes?"

He did not seem to find it an odd question, was quite ready to answer. "It's to the flat above the shoemaker's. Used to be a young couple in it."

"Do you know who's there now?"

"'Deed I don't. I've seen a dark woman going in but I haven't the foggiest who she is."

We went next to the shoemaker's. He was a hunchback. He came up to about our waists and I found it embarrassing to have to look at him straight on. His shop was gloomy, like a dark cave, and smelled thickly of leather and polishes. I sneezed. There were shoes everywhere. People had to make their shoes last longer in wartime, have them constantly soled and resoled.

"What is it, miss?" he demanded of Sally who had gone forward to his scored, pocked counter.

She said she thought her mother had said something about collecting a pair of shoes.

He peered up at her. "You the butcher's daughter?" She nodded. "No, there's nothing for you, miss. There was a pair of black courts last week but your mother collected them."

He looked as if he was about to shuffle off back to his workroom; he was not a man for a bit of crack the way many others were along the street. Sally had to summon her resources to hold him.

"Are you busy just now? I mean, I was wondering — I

28

think we may have other shoes to get mended. . ." Her voice trailed away.

Harriet stepped forward. She said that a friend of her mother's was looking for a flat, just a small one, and they had heard he had one which he sometimes rented. She was very good at thinking up plausible excuses on the spot. Perhaps a trait inherited from her father the lawyer.

He had a flat, he admitted, but it was rented out right now. Sally and Harriet leant their stomachs against the counter, I stayed behind. The shop wouldn't have held anyone else, not with all the boots and shoes as well.

It was rented to a foreigner, he volunteered, somewhat surprisingly.

"How interesting," said Harriet, sounding like her mother now. "French?"

"A Gerry, from the sound of her. Says her name's Berg. Miss Berg." I thought I saw a wicked glint come into his eye but could not be sure because of the gloom. "Up to no good, if you ask me."

"Really?" said Sally, also trying to sound like Mrs Linton.

I wondered why he had taken her as a tenant, if he had thought she was up to no good but it might have been rude to ask.

"She's — well, I don't know. . ." He shook his head.

"Furtive?" suggested Harriet. The word had cropped up in our English lesson that day and we felt it was a suitable adjective to ascribe to the object of our investigations.

He pursed his lips, considered. "Yes, that's right. Furtive."

"Does she have any friends?" asked Harriet.

"Not as I knows of but then I wouldn't see, would I? I'm in my back room with my boots all day."

We did not dare ask where he went at nights. I fancied he stayed in the back room and slept amongst the boots. Since he rented out the flat he probably wouldn't have had anywhere else to go.

He nodded to us, implying that he must go now, work called. He stroked his apron with long, amazingly slender hands. We shuffled out, calling loud goodbyes, as if we were more intimate with him that we were.

"Well!" said Harriet. "I think we've made quite a bit of progress."

I wouldn't have said it was much but at least we knew where she lived and that the shoemaker considered her furtive.

We ran down the street to the MacCabes' house, passing mine on the way. The light was on in my mother's sitting room and I could see a shadowy figure at the other side of the net curtaining. A customer having a fitting.

Mrs MacCabe clucked over our soaked heads but did not scold us with any real severity. Life to her seemed a matter for amusement. She loved a good laugh and often had it. "Away on upstairs to the bathroom and get yourselves dried off. You're like a lot of drowned rats."

After we had dried our heads and hung our coats on the pulley in the kitchen we retreated to Sally's bedroom, the smallest of the three in the house. Her parents slept in one and her four brothers in the other. The house was fair bursting at the seams, as Mrs MacCabe said, and they'd need either to move or put up a tent for the overflow in the back garden. Somehow, it was never the same once they did move to their big house with plenty of rooms for everybody and some left over.

Sally and I sat on her bed, Harriet had the pink and gold wicker chair. We took out our notebooks and sat with pencils poised. At that moment the door opened and in came Mrs MacCabe carrying a tray of steaming cocoa and coffee sponge cake.

"I thought you could all be doing with a bit of a warm up. You were looking quite blue when you came in, so you were." She handed out the cups which we received gratefully. I took a gulp of the hot chocolate and almost scalded my throat. Mrs MacCabe eyed the notebooks. "Doing your homework, are you?" She unearthed a packet of cigarettes from the depths of her apron pocket, took out a cigarette and lit it. She leant against the door jamb, smoking whilst she watched us eat. I think she thought Harriet and I weren't properly fed, she was always telling us we needed more beef on our bones. We didn't have to answer her question and she wouldn't have cared if we were making notes on the Lord Mayor himself. She thought Harriet and I were good for Sally, so Sally said: she considered us brainy and hoped some of our brains might rub off on her.

"Ma!" A voice called from behind.

"Oh, that'll be our Billy. 'Scuse me, girls!" She went off gaily, tripping down the stairs on her high high heels at which I marvelled. Sometimes we practised walking in her shoes and once I sprained my ankle. I told my mother I fell going down the kerb.

We drank the cocoa and ate the cake. A glow of contentment filled my stomach and I felt the edge taken off my zeal where following Fraulein Berg was concerned. Outside, the rain had turned to sleet.

"Now then," said Harriet, taking up her notebook and pencil again, "back to work, girls!" It was the cry we heard from Miss Bell if we as much as turned our heads to look out of the window.

We wrote our quarry's name at the top of page one. We were opening our file on Fraulein Berg. We realised we didn't know her Christian name but that should be easy enough to find out, said Harriet. On the second line we wrote: *Residence — Flat above shoemaker's shop.* Next: *Friends and acquaintances — None known. Previous habitation — Dublin, Eire.* It took up a few lines.

"We must now draw up a rota," said Harriet. "A watch." This was going to be less easy done than said for Harriet herself had many commitments after school, piano lessons, ballet lessons, elocution lessons. That left Sally and me to do most of the after school stretches and frequently I had to help my mother by running messages and getting the tea ready. And she was not keen on me being out after dark. The blackout covered a multitude of sins, she said, and tramps slept in the air raid shelter in the street.

Harriet became impatient. Where there was a will there was a way, she reminded us, which was the kind of little motto we were dished out at the Guides or Sunday School.

"Ah well, all right, we'll do what we can," said Sally. "And if we can't tail her all of the time it can't be helped."

We made up a rota as best we could. It was unfortunate that we would not be able to watch her for the main part of the evening since we considered she was bound to get involved in her most daring escapades under cover of darkness. I thought of Fraulein Berg's raw red hands rapping on the attaché case for attention. But of course we all knew it was the unlikeliest looking people who were spies. The other thing we decided to do was cross-question — as subtly as possible — all the surrounding shopkeepers and see if they had observed anything odd about their German neighbour.

And then Mrs MacCabe called us down to tea and the notebooks were tossed on to a heap on the bed.

We were ten at table, the seven MacCabes, Harriet and I, and Danny Forbes, a friend of Billy's. Danny was rather sweet on Harriet and Mr MacCabe teased them both, making her blush and Danny grin. Mrs MacCabe carried in plates heaped high with glistening brown sausages, rashers of bacon, fried eggs, potato bread and soda bread. What a feast! We tucked in and ate till I thought we must all burst. And at the back of us a huge fire roared up the chimney keeping the cold wet night at bay. When the first course was cleared away fresh plates came out laden with cakes, biscuits and scones, all home-baked and not with liquid paraffin either.

The giant teapot was replenished, everyone was urged to eat up. Mrs MacCabe wanted the table cleared, she declared. My mind boggled and my eyes goggled. A whole cherry cake had not yet been cut. The big knife was going into it now and a slice was falling, honey-coloured and bursting with bright red cherries.

"Come on, Katie," cried Mr MacCabe, "eat up! You're not a sparrow now, are you?"

He was such an agreeable man, most of the time, that you couldn't resist him. I took a piece of cake even though I didn't know where I would find room to put it. Sometimes, when Catholics were mentioned, which they seldom were in his house, he became quite bad-tempered and his face would grow dark. "They're all right as long as they keep their place," I'd heard him say, "but give them an inch and they'll take a mile." My mother said he was a bigot like many others she could name, though he was a kind man. After the 1941 bombings he had put free food into the mouths of Catholics as well as Protestants. His barking over religion was worse than his bite, she fancied, and as long as nothing serious crossed his life, like Sally wanting to marry a Catholic when she grew up, it was likely he would never get to the point of biting at all.

Anyway, we never gave a thought to his bigoted views that night, nor to Fraulein Berg either. It was only when Harriet and I went upstairs to collect our things to go home that we saw the tossed aside notebooks and remembered her.

I was on the first watch the following afternoon. I had to go home before I could do it. My mother would have been worried if I didn't, but we reckoned that Fraulein Berg would go home straight after school too. We saw her heading up the hill in front of us.

My mother was sewing a bridesmaid's dress in blue taffeta. She sat by the window where the light was better. The room was full of bales of material, silks and satins, tweeds and woollens, as it always was. I liked the colours of my mother's room but today I had no eyes for them.

"Have you any homework?" she asked, a routine question, after wanting to know if I'd had a good day.

"I'll do it later." I did not sit down. "Have you any messages you want done?"

"Don't you want something to eat first?" When I said I wasn't hungry she looked at me with surprise. "Were you in at Mr Dyson's on your road home?" I shrugged, indicating maybe I had been, maybe not. I jumped about restlessly, eyeing the mantlepiece clock. If I didn't get up the road soon, Fraulein Berg would have had time to take off for Berlin. Berlin. In my mind's eye I saw the hated Führer giving his salute from a dais and his steel-helmeted troops goose-stepping past below. I shivered.

"Have you got a cold, Kate? You must be careful now."

No, no, I interrupted, protesting. And what about her messages? I was not usually so keen to go shopping, she observed, snapping off the thread with her neat white teeth. She had lovely straight teeth, my mother. It was because she was not allowed to eat sweets as a girl, she told me, and I told her you'd need to be dead unlucky for your teeth to go rotten on the amount of sweets you got on the ration. She gave me hers most weeks.

Eventually I got out, with the shopping basket over my arm and my mother's worn leather purse in my pocket. She wanted a few things from the grocer's which suited me fine for the shop was right opposite the shoemaker's, and Fraulein Berg's flat.

The grocer was busy, which suited me too, as it gave me time to linger and keep an eye on the opposite side of the road. Mr MacMahon, bald head shining, stood behind the counter in his long brown coat. It took him a while to serve a customer, by the time he weighed out the sugar and rice and cut the butter and cheese with his big heavy knife. Little was pre-packaged.

Fraulein Berg had lit a table lamp by the window. I could see its golden glow and her head moving around behind it. Since it wasn't properly dark yet she didn't have to draw her blackout curtains. After a bit she sat down with her back to the window.

The woman in the queue in front of me lived in our street and was a well-known gossip. Mr MacMahon himself was not averse to hearing a bit of scandal, it was something to pass on to the next customer and liven up the day. They kept up a sequence of, "Do you tell me that now? Well, I never did!" "It's the Gospel truth." "Oh, I wouldn't be denying that for a second, not one. Mind you, she did always seem a bit. . ."

Fraulein Berg was sitting perfectly still, doing nothing, as far as I could judge. She was probably recovering from her day's ordeal at school. By the last period of the afternoon she looked like a wrung-out dish rag. Every now and then a double-decker trolley bus or a high truck went past and cut me off from her.

"What can I get you then, Kate?"

I spun round to realise that the other woman was humping her message bag out of the shop. I gave Mr MacMahon my mother's list and whilst he got the stuff together he blethered on to me asking about school and things like that. Across the road the lamp continued to burn.

"We've a new teacher. She's German and she lives across the road." I pointed.

He knew her, she had been in the shop, as I thought she might.

"Not much to say for herself," he commented, as he tucked in the ends of the brown paper bag. "One pound of rice, madam!"

I put the packet in my basket. "Does she ever talk to anyone else?"

"Can't say as I've seen her. Lonely life she leads, if you ask me."

There didn't seem to be much more to be gleaned from him but still I hovered for it was warm in the shop — he had a paraffin heater on at the back — and it would be cold in the street. I was supposed to watch her till tea-time and, according to Harriet, note down her every movement. I had to move when the next customer appeared.

I walked two shops along to the haberdasher's and looked in the window. When next I turned to look up at Fraulein Berg's flat I saw that her head was no longer where it had been for the last ten minutes. I crossed the road.

There was a bus stop near her door so I hung about there as if I might be waiting for a bus. I kept hoping that somebody

I knew would appear so that I would have an excuse to stand chatting but of course when you want someone or something to turn up they never do. From films I had the idea that the thing to do was to lean against a lamp post reading a newspaper, but if anyone came past and saw me propped up with the *Belfast Telegraph* in front of me they'd think I'd gone loopy. Obviously, tailing a suspect was no cushy job and not one the police would fight over to get. Before then I had imagined it would be glamorous and exciting to have to tail someone: I had seen myself flattening my body against walls, dodging cars in a busy street, hailing taxis. I thought of Sally and Harriet inside their nice warm houses, eating, more than likely. I was starving, having missed my after-school snack.

One or two people who knew my mother passed, said hello, and looked at me curiously. I was beginning to feel I must be standing out like a sore thumb bound up with ten yards of bandages. I moved closer to Fraulein Berg's door. Nothing very revealing about that. It didn't even have her name on it. And I couldn't very well look through the letter box, not right here on the main street.

Suddenly, the door opened and I almost fell inward.

"Kathleen! I thought I heard someone at the door. Were you knocking?"

"No, no, 'twasn't me. It wasn't anybody." I started to talk very rapidly. I hadn't known she lived here, I said, I'd just been taking a rest after coming out of the shops. My face felt like a boiled beetroot newly taken out of its skin.

"Ah. It must have been the wind then."

"I wouldn't be a bit surprised. It is quite windy today."

She hesitated, before saying, "Would you like to come up for a cup of tea?"

I hesitated now. Take tea with the Enemy? That sounded like treason. Or did she want to lure me inside? *Come into my parlour, said the spider to the fly.* But it would be a chance to get inside her flat, and that was a bit of luck we had never bargained on. I could imagine Sally's and Harriet's faces when I told them I'd actually been inside!

"Thank you very much," I said, all prim and proper now. "That would be very nice."

I followed her up a narrow flight of linoleum-covered stairs to her flat. She was wearing thick lisle stockings and her legs were very thin. The flat consisted of two small rooms — bedroom and living room — with a tiny kitchenette and bathroom.

"But I am very pleased with it," she said, smiling. "It is a home to have."

It looked pretty bleak to me with its floors also covered with linoleum and the walls with faded autumn-leaf paper, splotched at intervals with greasy looking stains. And it was almost as cold as the street. A one bar electric fire glowed in the grate.

"Sit down, Kathleen. Take your coat off, dear. I will boil the kettle."

I took the chair beside the fire, at her insistence. The springs went down with a twang as I sat. Whilst she was in the kitchenette I had a good look at the room. There were one or two books on a shelf, and a pile of exercise books, presumably waiting to be corrected, were lying on the table, but there was nothing much else to see, apart from the few bits of furniture. No photographs. Not a single one. Odd that. Unless she kept them in her bedroom. Our house was cluttered with photographs of cousins and aunts, ourselves, my father, and every ledge had a piece of china or some other kind of bric-a-brac perched on it. We had presents from Portrush, Dun Laoghaire, Blackpool, and the Isle of Man, brought back by customers of my mother. Would I have expected her to have had presents from Cologne or the Black Forest on display? I wasn't sure. She might have them hidden away in drawers.

She put her head round the door. "I'm just going to get

some biscuits from Mr MacMahon."

"Please don't bother," I was about to say, but she was already gone. I listened to her feet on the stairs, then the bottom door closed.

I jumped up, went to the window. I watched her crossing the road, dodging a bicycle. She had not bothered to put on her coat. There seemed to be two or three people waiting at the grocer's counter so she would be gone for a few minutes. It was my big chance to search her flat. To search? Could I really do that? Harriet would say certainly, all was fair, in love or war. And I was unlikely to get another opportunity.

I went into the bedroom. The air felt glacial, as if it had never been heated in its life. There were no photographs or knicknacks here either. On a chair beside the bed stood a travelling alarm clock and a book. The book was a German novel by Thomas Mann, but it had been published in Britain. I flicked through the pages: they contained no loose sheets, no messages, no underlinings. Gingerly, I opened the wardrobe door. Inside hung a dark brown dress and a dark blue one. She was wearing a black one today, with a grey cardigan. That seemed to be her total wardrobe, as far as top clothes were concerned, apart from her black coat. I supposed she would have to travel light, to make a quick getaway, if necessary. I put out my hand, looked at the inside of the blue dress and saw the utility label which meant that she had purchased it in this country. The other dress had the label of a Dublin shop. I closed the door. I took a quick look in the drawers, my heart hammering furiously against my chest as I did so, for every moment I expected to hear her quiet voice and light footstep behind me.

Returning to the living room, I let out a long sigh of relief.

The books on her shelf were mostly in German — one or two were English — but all had been published in London.

Inside the fly leaf of one was written Hildegarde Berg. *Hildegarde*. So now we knew her Christian name. She didn't have a single thing in her flat that had come from Germany, as far as I could gather. Very strange, Harriet and Sally agreed, when I told them. Only to be expected, said Harriet: she would not carry incriminating evidence about with her.

I was just about to sit down when I noticed two letters lying on the mantlepiece. One bore an Eire stamp and a Dublin postmark, the other had been posted in Belfast. I eased the sheet of paper out of the Dublin envelope, and saw that it was covered with German script which looked as intelligible to me as Chinese. The door down below was opening. Hastily I replaced the letters and re-arranged myself in the chair, trying to look innocent. I didn't feel at all innocent but she didn't seem to notice. She was carrying a bag of biscuits.

"Broken biscuits. I hope you don't mind?"

"No, no," I assured her. "We often have broken biscuits."

I almost choked trying to get down half a pink cream sandwich biscuit and half a chocolate Bourbon. I washed the crumbs over my dry throat with the thick stewed tea, shaking my head as she offered me the plate again.

"Mr MacMahon is very nice?" she said.

I nodded. I couldn't think of any conversation to make so she laboured on, asking about the shopkeepers, and whether I liked reading. My answers were all in monosyllables, or else given by nods or shakes of the head. She must have been astonished for I had plenty to say for myself in the classroom, as I was frequently told.

Eventually, I picked up my shopping bag and said I'd need to be going, my mother would be waiting for her messages.

"Of course! I have been thoughtless, I have kept you."

"It's all right, really."

We almost fell over one another in our awkwardness. On

the way to the door I stopped in front of the window. "You've got a good view of the street." It was one that I would not have minded myself: I liked to see things going on.

Fraulein Berg nodded. "Yes, I like it. It's nice to watch the buses pass full of people who are going somewhere."

It was only then that I realised exactly where she was situated. Right opposite the A.R.P. Post, which was above the MacMahons' shop. With a pair of binoculars... But she didn't have a pair of binoculars, not unless she kept them under the bed. Later, Harriet said I was an idiot not to have looked under the bed first *and* the mattress.

Fraulein Berg was waiting to see me out. I followed her down the dimly lit staircase and, as she opened the door, she shivered, saying she hated winter. She would love to live in a hot climate. "One day, who knows?" She smiled. She looked as if she had forgotten me.

"Goodbye, Fraulein Berg. And thank you for a lovely tea."

I wheeled about and bumped into Miss Thistlethwaite coming out of the shoemaker's with her dog. I had a knack of being caught red-handed, whereas Harriet had one of evading detection, of sliding round the corner just in time. On one occasion, when I went to the pictures with Billy MacCabe on a Saturday afternoon and the lights came up at the interval, I realised that I was sitting next to the headmistress. I had to pretend Billy had nothing to do with me and kept up a conversation with Miss Thistlethwaite that ran, "You here on your own, Kathleen?" "Yes, Miss Thistlethwaite." "Does your mother not mind you going to the cinema alone?" "No, Miss Thistlethwaite." After two minutes Billy couldn't stifle his giggles any longer. He also gave me a hefty kick on the shin which made me cry out loudly.

"And where have you been, Kathleen?" asked Miss Thistlethwaite.

I presumed she knew where all her staff lived so there did not seem much point in lying. "I've been to tea with Fraulein Berg."

"To tea? With Fraulein — " She was unable to finish. "Did she invite you?"

As if I would invite myself! "Yes, Miss Thistlethwaite."

She pursed her lips. She disapproved of staff and pupils hobnobbing outside school hours. There was the time when the domestic science teacher asked a Sixth Form girl to tea and had been ticked off sharply. So the teacher had whispered to the girl next day, saying that she was sorry but she could not invite her to come again. Miss Thistlethwaite had said it was not seemly for a member of staff to entertain a pupil. We had looked up the word in the dictionary. It appeared that it was not becoming, suitable or decent for a pupil to drink tea with a teacher.

We parted, Miss Thistlethwaite and I, and I knew that that would be the first and last time I would take tea with Fraulein Berg.

It was always a Saturday when we were invited to tea at the Lintons. A quite different affair from a MacCabe tea-party, of course. For a start, the Lintons, Mr and Mrs, were usually going out and so we had tea, the three of us on our own, which we liked as it gave us a chance to chat unrestrained inside. Most of our unrestrained chatting had to be done in the cold and wet.

This Saturday they were going to a cocktail party from six till eight.

"We shall leave at half-past five, Harriet," said her mother. "And we shall be back not long after eight, if not before. The tea is laid in the dining room for you, girls."

"Thank you, Mrs Linton," Sally and I chorused.

The whole house smelled of Jasmine essence whilst the water was running for her bath. I decided that when I grew up I was going to buy that essence by the jarful: it would make me feel glamorous just to smell like that.

We sat in Harriet's bedroom which was a big square room with twin beds and two easy chairs. We could lounge at leisure here and did, our notebooks on our knees. They were beginning to fill up a little. Now we knew the Fraulein's

Christian name and her address; and we had a full description of her wardrobe and possessions and a list of everyone she had been seen speaking to in the two weeks we'd been covering her. The grocer, the ironmonger, Mrs McCurdy, the postman. Hardly a very helpful list, I observed, but Harriet said that one expected to proceed slowly at the beginning, that watching a suspect was a task that required patience but would be rewarded by a breakthrough at some point. We knew all the jargon.

"The main thing is that we are building up a picture of her activities."

Her activities, as far as we had been able to discern so far, consisted of going to school, coming home, buying a few groceries at Mr MacMahon's and then going upstairs to have tea by herself at the window. She had also been observed going to the postbox with letters, but since we didn't have X-Ray eyes we couldn't see to whom the letters were addressed. Sally had tried squinting through the letter box and been ticked off by the man who ran the post office. And Harriet had managed to engage the postman in conversation and find out that she got a letter once a week regularly with an Eire postmark.

"Pity you didn't have time to see what was inside that other letter, Kate. The one with the Belfast postmark. It might be her contact here."

I thought I'd done pretty well, considering, and said so.

"Course you did," said Sally. "I'd have been terrified if it had been me. Let's have a dance, shall we?"

We were trying to learn to do the tango. Harriet put a record on her gramophone, cranked the handle, and to the strains of *Lady of Spain* she and Sally attempted to glide around the room in what they considered to be South American style. Sally kept tripping on Harriet's toes. Harriet led; she held her partner's hand firmly, bending her over so that her back arched and her hair almost touched the ground.

44

"One, two, three, four, Sally!" commanded Harriet. She had an advantage when it came to dancing, due to all that ballet training.

We didn't hear Mrs Linton coming in. She looked a little disconcerted for a moment but her smile returned quickly and she said, "What are you girls up to then?" She was wearing an emerald-green velvet cocktail dress, made by my mother. She was a bit on the plump side, had a heavy shelf for a bosom, but she did look rather good in the dress.

"You look fantastic, Mrs Linton," said Sally, who found it easier to hand out compliments than I did.

"Thank you, Sally dear. How nice of you! We're off now, Harriet."

Mr Linton put his head round the door to say goodbye and issue last instructions and warnings. We must make sure the cooker was turned off. We must keep the front and back doors locked and not answer either. And we must not, on any account, leave the house until they returned.

As soon as their car drove away, we ran down to the dining room and Harriet lifted the cloth that had been laid over the food. The meal was more delicately prepared and set out than the one we had at the MacCabes, but it was delicious in its own way. We had dozens of little sandwiches cut into triangles just as Mrs Linton did them for her bridge parties, sausage rolls, pancakes, chocolate finger biscuits, and a walnut cake that had come from Fullers in Dublin. We didn't bother to waste time making tea, we drank water instead.

"I don't think we'd better eat *all* the cake," said Harriet. "Mother will expect to have some left for tomorrow."

"I'm going to Dublin at half-term," said Sally, as she munched her way through a thick slice, walnuts spilling sideways out of her mouth. What gluttons we were every chance we got! "Mum's taking me for a birthday treat."

"Lucky you!" I had never been to Dublin, but Sally and

Harriet went regularly, coming back with tales of how much real cream and how many boxes of milk chocolates they had consumed. Although there was some rationing in the South, it was not anywhere near as severe as ours and you could get pretty well anything you wanted if you were prepared to pay for it. But apart from the food, I was dying to see O'Connell Street with Nelson's statue in the middle and Phoenix Park and the Liffey and the Germans who were reputed to be walking about as bold as brass talking to one another in loud German. There was still an embassy there and Mr MacCabe, who didn't have much time for the Eire Government, said the Southern Irish were hoping for a German victory. On her last visit Sally had almost got run over by a van belonging to the Swastika Laundry. The van actually had a big black swastika on its side — that most hated of emblems! — and she was sure it had been the sight of that which had taken her breath away and almost got her knocked down.

"Maybe you could come with us, Kate. I'm sure Mum wouldn't mind."

I shrugged. I didn't see that as a possibility: I knew my mother could not afford the money and the MacCabes spent plenty when they went, staying in a fine hotel and stocking up on clothes and all sorts of things that were not so easy to come by in the North, even on the Black Market.

We almost cleared the plates, leaving only a few biscuits and half of the walnut cake. We staggered into the kitchen and washed the dishes, then foxtrotted up and down the terrazzo floor to work off the over-full feeling in our stomachs.

"What'll we do now?" said Sally, when we'd had enough of that.

What would we like to do? Harriet enquired. Play Monopoly, cards, listen to records? She was always very polite when we were at her house, played the hostess as to the manner born.

We did not fancy any of those things. We were restless.

"We could go and see what Fraulein Berg is up to," suggested Harriet.

"But your mother said not to go out," said Sally.

"As long as we're back before they are it won't matter, will it?"

We were only too ready to agree. And now that we had the idea of going out we could not bear to stay in. We rushed for our coats. Harriet found a torch in the hallstand drawer. We left by the back door after carefully going round the house switching off every light and checking that nothing was on that shouldn't be. Harriet locked the door, tugged it to make sure it was closed, and pocketed the key.

"Don't lose it," I cautioned.

But I should not worry about details like that where Harriet was concerned: she had never lost a key in her life, unlike Sally and I who had lost so many that our mothers refused to give us any more.

We had about a mile to go to the main road. Harriet walked in the middle, shining the torch downward so that enemy aircraft passing overhead would not think we were signalling to them. The first part of the walk was a bit scarifying on a dark moonless night with not even a star to flash out a little light overhead: the road was tree-lined, and the houses hemmed in by hedges higher than our heads. In the bare branches of the trees the wind sighed and moaned like an old woman keening. We moved in closer to Harriet and the torch. I was glad I didn't live so far away from the main road where cars and people were always going to and fro. It was no wonder Harriet wasn't allowed out at night on her own.

Then we came to the semis, and here, already, there was a bit more life and movement: a man was walking his dog, two women stood blethering at a gate, a couple of kids were peeping from an upstairs window defying the blackout. We went smartly past this stretch, not wishing to bump into a

MacCabe and be asked where did we think we were going? Even from the pavement you could hear there was noise inside their house. We didn't loiter going by my house either, not that it was likely that my mother would be standing in the doorway leaning against the jamb to watch the night. That was not her style at all. She had a reputation for keeping herself to herself. She said she was too busy to do anything else and, besides, other people took enough from her during the course of their fitting and measuring sessions. By the time the day was done she was content to sit by the fire and read or listen to the wireless, or, once a week, go to the pictures. She always took me with her, either on a Friday or a Saturday night. It was our big treat of the week. I was crazy about the cinema, would have gone twice a week if I could, for the programme changed Mondays and Thursdays, but there was not enough money for that.

They were singing in the gospel hall. Once, Sally and I had gone in for a lark but it had turned out to be kind of dreary, with nothing but hymns and prayers about sin and repentance and people pestering us to be saved. Now and then I met one of the women in the street and she would ask me if I'd seen the light yet? The message on the board outside tonight was: *Sinner, flee from the wrath to come!* I looked away quickly. The messages often seemed to be written up just for me.

At last we reached the main road.

We turned right and, conscious that we were nearing the enemy, walked more stealthily, keeping close to the shuttered shops, not speaking. Harriet put out the torch. And then we leapt backward in disarray — our history teacher was always talking about armies being in disarray — for the door of Fraulein Berg's flat had opened no more than five yards ahead of us. She came out in her black coat. She walked to the bus stop and stood at the back of a line of four or five people. We withdrew into the doorway of the MacCabes' shop.

"She must be going out," whispered Sally.

"Obviously," said Harriet. "We must follow her."

"Can we?"

"Why not? I've got some money. Have you two?"

We each found we had something in the bottom of our pockets. I had got my pocket money that morning and had only spent a part of it in Mr Dyson's.

We saw the dipped lights of a trolley bus approaching.

"Are gou game?" asked Harriet.

"Sure," we said.

"Lead on, MacDuff!" I cried.

We waited till the queue moved into the body of the bus. Fraulein Berg was last to board. As she put her foot on to the platform we sidled out of our hiding place. And as soon as she reached a seat, we flung ourselves at the bus which was starting to glide away from the stop. I was last. I almost fell but Sally grabbed my arm and hauled me aboard. We raced up the stairs to the top deck.

We had the top of the bus to ourselves. After the conductor had been up for our fares and given us a little lecture on jumping on to buses when they were moving, we were able to hang over the top of the stair well and keep an eye on the platform below. We took it in turns, doing five minutes at a stretch, which was long enough as the blood rushed to our heads and made us feel dizzy. After all the food we'd eaten I was feeling a bit sick as well.

The bus stopped at almost every stop and each time it did the one on watch went a few steps down the stairs to get a better view. Half-way into town two or three men came up but they went to the front and did not seem to be interested in our antics.

"She must be going right into the centre," I said.

"We must keep watch though," said Harriet. "We could easily lose her. And then where would we be?"

"Going to the City Hall on our own," giggled Sally.

Fraulein Berg did, in fact, stay on the bus until it reached the City Hall, which is right in the middle of the city centre and was as far as the bus went.

"Are you lot staying on for the night?" called up the conductor.

We clattered down the stairs — we had been waiting till Fraulein Berg would move further up the pavement. She only went a few yards and then joined another queue at a different bus stop.

"Oh, well," said Harriet. "In for a penny in for a pound. We've got to see it through now."

The next bus was going up the Antrim Road to Cavehill. It was not an area we knew well, except for the zoo and Cave Hill itself, where sometimes in summer we went for picnics. She could hardly be going to either, but Harriet said we didn't know, did we? The Cave Hill would be dark and lonely and a good place for secret meetings.

"She might be going to the Floral Hall," giggled Sally. It was a dance hall.

"Don't be daft," said Harriet.

I began to giggle too, imagining Fraulein Berg doing the tango, a rose between her teeth.

The top deck was quite crowded this time and we were not able to get the back seat which meant that every time we came to a stop one of us had to get up and run to the top of the stairs. It meant too that we got in people's way. Gradually, the bus began to empty. We were drawing nearer and nearer to the terminus and still the straight-backed, black-coated figure could be seen sitting on the bottom deck whenever we went to check. Once, when I was spying on her, she turned round and frowned, and I ducked back just in time. At least, I hoped it was in time. I didn't think she'd seen me. But may be she sensed she was being watched.

"She might be going to the zoo," said Sally, as we sped onward through the black night.

"It'll be shut," said I.

"But they can't shut Cave Hill, can they now?" said Harriet.

We were so busy gassing we almost missed her getting off.

"Quick!" cried Sally. "She's getting off."

We hurtled down the stairs. The bus was moving away gathering speed. We jumped.

"Do you want to bleeding well kill yourselves?" yelled the conductor after us.

Fortunately, Fraulein Berg had begun to walk on and seemed to be unaware of what had happened behind her. Her thoughts were probably on other things: dangerous things. Sally picked herself up and dusted herself down. I rubbed my ankle tenderly: I thought I'd sprained it. Harriet, of course, had landed on her feet. Ballet training again. Perhaps Sally and I should take a few lessons to get us into shape for jumping on and off moving buses. It seemed desirable training for secret service agents.

"Hurry up," said Harriet, "or we'll lose her."

She had turned down a side street and was gone from our sight, but we soon caught her up. In front of her she carried her torch, discreetly held down, and so we followed the little bobbing light, staying about twenty yards behind it. She turned down one street after another, walking with a steady measured pace that suggested she could keep going all night. Each dark suburban street looked the same: we paid them no heed, had eyes only for the dark figure with the light ahead. We heard the ring of her steps in the quiet misty air. It was quite misty, a fact which had surprised us when we got off the bus as it had been clear on our side of town and in the centre.

"Probably because it's near the hill," whispered Harriet.

We walked on tiptoe, as best we could, and kept close to the hedge into which we could flatten ourselves should she turn and come back. The hedges felt prickly and damp and I was glad that we didn't have to resort to that strategy.

Without warning, she wheeled sharply into a driveway. The light bobbed between shrubs and came to rest against a door. We nipped across the road. We could see the dark figure of the Fraulein against the vague outline of a bungalow.

"Let's go closer," said Harriet softly. "She won't see us in this fog."

We crept back across the road and positioned ourselves by the gate of the house next door. Fraulein Berg was still waiting: the light was steady. When the door opened we craned our heads round the corner and listened intently.

A woman had answered the door and was greeting her visitor warmly, embracing her on both cheeks the way that Continentals do. And they were speaking German!

Fraulein Berg stepped into the lighted hall and the door closed. We were left in the dark again.

"You didn't hear what they said, did you?" asked Sally.

I could just about manage *Guten Morgen, Guten Tag,* and *Auf Wiedersehen,* and I knew they hadn't said any of those things.

"We haven't found out much, have we?" Sally sounded disappointed, but Harriet was not despondent. We had found out one contact, hadn't we? And we knew where she lived. Harriet crept up the path to see the number on the door. *Number twenty-seven,* we wrote in our notebooks. And then we went back along to the beginning of the road to find its name and we wrote that down too.

Suddenly, Harriet had an idea. We could call at another house and ask if a Mrs Carson lived there. I felt uneasy at the idea of my mother's name being dragged into this but it wasn't my mother's name particularly, said Harriet: it was just the first name that came in to her mind.

"But she won't live there," objected Sally.

"It would be funny if she did," said I.

Harriet decided on number seventeen. We traipsed up the

path and she rang the doorbell. She had a great deal of courage, had Harriet. Sally and I, standing on the step behind her, were glad not to be in the front line.

A man in a fawn cardigan opened the door. We could hear Henry Hall and his Orchestra playing in the background.

"Yes?"

"We're looking for people called Carson."

"Sorry, miss. Not here." He made to close the door, obviously keen to get back to his wireless.

"You wouldn't know where they might live, would you? Perhaps it's number twenty-seven."

"No, it's not twenty-seven." He shook his head.

"Are you sure?"

"They're called O'Malley in that house."

He went back to Henry Hall, we retreated down the drive. You could not get much more of an Irish name than O'Malley. It was a Republican name though, said Sally, not so much an Ulster one.

"You're right, Sally," said Harriet. "You've got a point there."

"But there are Republicans in the North," I said.

"Quite," said Harriet. "And this lot are probably harbouring a German spy."

We got out our notebooks and entered the name *O'Malley* opposite *number twenty-seven*, standing behind a hedge to do so and two of us taking a turn to shine the torch for the others. Now it was time to head home.

Harriet said she remembered the way; she led. From one street we went in to another, sometimes coming back to the same streets again, when we would realise that we had encircled a crescent or executed a triangle. The mist was deepening; from the Lough came the distant sound of the fog-horn. We went round and round, not the mulberry bush, but a maze of suburban streets in North Belfast. Sally and I knew fairly quickly that we were lost but it took quite a while and a few turns around a few more blocks — some dark trees were beginning to assume familiar shapes — before Harriet was prepared to halt and admit it.

She beamed the torch on to her wrist watch. "Crumbs," she said, "it's half-past eight!"

All hell was let loose at the Lintons' when they returned to find the house empty: those were the words Mr MacCabe used to describe it, though he possibly exaggerated as the Lintons were not the kind of people to start screaming and yelling. They were more likely to pace up and down and give vent to their anger in a controlled sort of way. It was easy enough for us to visualize what had taken place.

They came in at ten minutes past eight and were surprised, on opening the front door and calling out Harriet's name, to receive no reply. There had been only one light on, in the hall, and the back door was locked. They called in the garden, looked in the garage, the garden shed, the dug-out air raid shelter that Mr Linton had sweated over in the autumn of 1939. We were not of course to be found. But Harriet knew perfectly well she was not allowed out after dark unaccompanied by an adult and Mr Linton had given us all special instructions not to leave the house. It was most puzzling.

At half-past eight they rang the MacCabes. No, the girls were not there, they were told. "They might have gone to the chip shop," suggested Mrs MacCabe, just about giving

Mr Linton apoplexy. Harriet was forbidden to go in to the chip shop, her parents considering it to be unsavoury and common. I found it most savoury and Sally and I went there, as often as we could, frequently bringing out a bag of chips for Harriet. We would then scuttle into a side alley where we would devour them rapidly as though we hadn't eaten for a week. Harriet was not supposed to eat anything in the street, not even a sweet, although almost every day we were to be seen coming along the road sucking ice cream.

My mother, not being on the telephone, could not be rung up but Mrs MacCabe sent Billy round to see if we were there. No, said my mother, we were not there, and she had not seen me since three o'clock that afternoon. But we might have gone to the cinema café, she suggested, if we had any money to spend, even though I was not supposed to go there in the evenings without her. But she knew us well enough to realise that we might sometimes do things we were not supposed to do. The message was relayed back to the Lintons who did not receive it kindly either. The cinema café! By this time they must have been deciding that Sally and I were most unsuitable friends for their daughter. They were always trying to bring Harriet together with other nice little girls, daughters of friends, fellow ballet dancers, but so far without success.

At nine o'clock Mr Linton tried ringing the MacCabes again. The line was engaged. Mrs MacCabe was talking to her sister, Nell, about her proposed visit to Dublin at half-term and Nell thought she wouldn't mind going as well. They always spoke on the phone for hours, those two, once they got going. Mr Linton tried another three times, then he and his wife drove up to the MacCabes' house. Mrs MacCabe was still on the telephone when Billy opened the door to them. She waved them in from where she sat on the hallstand.

They were in quite a state, she told Sally afterwards, and it was that which made them a bit uneasy too. Normally they didn't worry when Sally was out for an extra half-hour, especially if she was with me whom they considered sensible. Mr MacCabe came from the living room in his shirt sleeves, his braces hanging down. He was feeling irritable. He had been drinking beer and having a game of cards with his brother, George. It was Saturday night and he could have seen Sally far enough.

"Have you tried the chip shop?" asked Mrs MacCabe, still holding the receiver in her hand, keeping her sister on the end of the line.

The Lintons had not but decided that they had better do it now. They went to the chip shop, saw no sign of us in the queue, so Mr Linton went in and asked the man if he had seen three girls that evening, one with long blond hair, the others medium-length, one brown, one black. The chip man held out his hands and shrugged in his best Italian manner. He saw many girls every evening, of all colours of hair, of all lengths. If Mr Linton had asked him if Sally and Kate had been in, he'd have got a more definite answer.

From there he went to the cinema café and searched the faces at the tables. He asked a waitress if she'd seen us but she was too busy to stop. The service was dreadful at the café: they had two waitresses for all the tables and you usually had to wait hours to be served.

By then it was half-past nine.

"Something must have happened to them, Charles," said his wife. (Sally and I used to re-enact this bit afterwards, amusing ourselves, pretending to be Mrs Linton ready to swoon.)

At that point he decided it was time to call out the police.

Meanwhile, back on the north side of the town, Sally and Harriet and I were trudging homewards through the fog. We had bumped into a constable on the beat and asked him the way to the City Hall so he had escorted us to the main road and told us to follow our noses. Our intention had been to take a bus but when we counted up our money we realised we didn't have enough left for the three of us. When we'd set out on Fraulein Berg's trail we hadn't bargained on having to take so many buses.

"You go on the bus, Harriet," I said. "Sally and I'll walk."

But Harriet absolutely refused to leave us. "United we stand," she declared. "Divided we fall."

We set off, arms linked, for the long walk. It must be at least three or four miles, we reckoned. An hour's fast march, said Harriet, forcing us along at a spanking pace. We did not ask what her parents would be thinking. We did not think about them. We did not think about Fraulein Berg either. The night absorbed us, the overcast sky, the dark shapes of buildings, passing cars and buses; and the feel of the hard pavement beneath our feet. I had put on my best shoes to go to tea at the Lintons; the soles were cardboard thin and they were not comfortable to wear for any length of time so it was not long till my feet were hurting. I did not mention it until Sally said her feet were killing her.

"Think of the soldiers marching into battle with torn boots and bleeding feet," said Harriet.

Our history teacher had been telling us about the troops on the run from Napoleon floundering their way back into the snowy wastes of Russia with empty stomachs, rags on their backs, and no boots at all on their feet. At least our stomachs were not empty, although when we passed a chip shop our noses twitched and our eyes swivelled left for a glimpse of the inside of the lighted shop as the door swung open and a crowd of youths came out carrying newspaper parcels.

"Want a chip, girls?" called out one boy.

Harriet hastened us on, her head held high. She had a marvellously straight back and sometimes Sally and I practised walking up and down with books on our heads but it didn't seem to make any difference. Every time we passed boys hanging around street corners — street-corner boys, we called them — she tilted her head higher. They usually whistled. "Cheek," she would say.

After the first mile or two our feet were beginning to lag. We sang to encourage ourselves along and keep our spirits up. Armies often sang as they marched, said Harriet, although I thought they would have been better saving their breath for the fighting. We sang, *Pack up your troubles in your old kit bag and smile, smile, smile!* That was a good tune to walk to, one we had marched to before, on Girl Guide hikes. "What's the use of worrying, it never was worth while," we sang lustily and fervently, thinking that the man who had written that had known what he was talking about.

A drunk man lurched out of the shadows in front of us and we had to break rank to avoid him. Drunks were harmless, said Sally, they hadn't the strength or the wit to be anything else. We saw a few, it being Saturday night. Passing pubs, we heard lots of loud noise and laughter. "Sounds jolly," said Sally. "Pity we can't go in." Harriet said women did not go into public houses, and nor did many men either, come to that. Come to Mr Linton, we supposed, for he was not the type you saw reeling out of a pub on a Saturday night. We put him from our minds.

"Another song!" cried Sally.

"Sally, Sally, pride of our alley," I crooned and Sally collapsed in laughter, falling over Harriet's feet. But Harriet took up Gracie Field's famous song and so too did Sally, and the three of us delivered a rendering that could only be described as terrible. We screeched on the high notes, were madly out of tune even on the low ones. "You mean more than the whole world to me!" We finished up, letting our voices rip.

"The Lord save us," said a man going by.

We amused ourselves at any rate. The song had made us feel slightly light-headed, that and being out on a Saturday night after dark. In fact, in spite of the state of our feet, we were thoroughly enjoying ourselves. Like condemned men eating hearty breakfasts.

From Gracie Fields we moved to Vera Lynn, the 'Forces' sweetheart'. We sang, *There'll be bluebirds over the white cliffs of Dover, tomorrow just you wait and see*, and *I'll be seeing you in all the old familiar places*. They were not such good rhythms to walk to, unless we speeded them up which we did, until they emerged like a sound track run riot. More hilarity followed.

"Come on, you two," urged Harriet. "Keep moving."

"My throat's dry," said Sally.

There was nothing to be done about that. The money in our pockets wouldn't buy anything except one bus fare. We decided to give our throats a rest from singing although I couldn't say we stopped talking. We were never quiet for one step of the road. We got on to one of our favourite topics: films and film stars. We were all mad about American films, not so much British ones which we found dull by comparison. We were mad about anything American. We saw America as the land of freedom and plenty and bright lights that shone the night through. The MacCabes kept getting food and clothing parcels from relatives in New Jersey and Wyoming — not that they needed them but then the relatives wouldn't realise that — and sometimes they'd put in a bundle of magazines. We pored over the magazines, reading every ad, and decided that we would emigrate when we grew up. Life over there was obviously a far more glamorous and exciting affair than it was in deadly dull old Belfast where nothing exciting ever happened and it rained ninety-nine days out of every hundred.

"Something exciting has happened now," Harriet pointed out. "A spy has been dropped into our midst. And we had good weather the whole time we were at Portstewart last July." The Lintons always went to Portstewart, a resort on the Antrim coast, to the same hotel, where they knew the 'crowd'. The MacCabes usually went away for days 'here and there', sometimes squashing me in amongst them, but the rest of our holidays we spent at home. We went to the outdoor concerts called 'Holidays at Home' where people tapdanced on postage-sized platforms and sang songs like *I'm a rambler, I'm a gambler.*

"But you still want to be a film star, don't you?" said Sally. "And go to Hollywood?"

Our hopes for one of us making it to Hollywood were pinned on Harriet. We saw her as a cross between Ginger Rogers (because of her dancing) and Betty Grable (because of her long legs). Betty Grable's legs were insured for millions of dollars, we had read in one of the magazines. In these journals we gleaned all manner of information and bits of advice.

"Imagine I'm Fred Astaire," said Sally, holding out her arms.

Harriet passed me the torch and I pirouetted the light around their feet whilst they glided up and down the pavement. I hummed for them and when they whirled back beside me, Harriet curtsied low to Sally.

"Thank you, Ginge. You dance divinely."

Our progress home was, obviously, none too fast.

When Harriet went to Hollywood, Sally and I would accompany her as her managers. We could rent, or buy, one of those dream houses up on Beverley Hills with leopard skin rugs on the floors, a cocktail bar in the corner, and a swimming pool in the garden. It was the swimming pool that I fancied most of all. It would be a far cry from the public, chlorinated one we went to where the kids yelled and the noise reverberated under the glass roof until it gave you a headache. I always came out with a sore head and red eyes. I was a keen swimmer and to tell the truth I wouldn't have minded being a film star myself, of the Esther Williams variety, wearing a white bathing costume and a red flower behind my ear, gliding up and down a turquoise-green pool to the strains of sweet music, whilst Gregory Peck hung admiringly over the edge. I didn't admit my ambition to Sally or Harriet though. They might have laughed. I didn't look like film star material.

The ground was beginning to look familiar.

"Donegall Place coming up!" cried Sally.

We were on our last stretch to the City Hall. If it had been daylight we would have been able to see the big white building ahead with its green copper domes. Everything seemed to happen round it: streets converged, as did thousands of starlings, and people waited for buses or something to turn up.

A number of American soldiers were hanging about. You could tell them from quite a distance away by their pork pie hats. G.I.s. There were always some about for they were stationed in Northern Ireland whilst they waited to go to the Front. They were waiting to invade Europe, said Mr MacCabe, (I thought he shouldn't have said so out loud since we had been warned that walls have ears), along with the British Forces of course, and the sooner they got on with it the better. The way he talked about it you'd have thought there was nothing more to it than nipping across the city and back. Sally's cousin was engaged to a G.I. and was going off to live in Tennessee when the war ended. We envied her from the bottom of our hearts and planned to visit her at the first opportunity. We often talked about the trip and imagined ourselves sailing into New York harbour seeing the Statue of Liberty and the skyscrapers standing up against the brilliant blue sky. We were dying to see a skyscraper. Imagine a building a hundred storeys high! We craned our necks backward trying to imagine it, and couldn't.

A G.I. whistled at Harriet who, in the distance and a bad light, looked much older than she was. She swished her hair disdainfully about her shoulders and the torch light jerked from side to side.

A clock began to strike. We halted, in mid-pavement, to count the strokes. We had forgotten that time existed.

"Ten," breathed Harriet, as the last stroke trembled in the air and died. "Crikes! *They'll* be climbing the wall." It was the first time she had mentioned *them*.

I suggested she use the money to phone home. We had to wait five minutes outside a box whilst a man talked to his girl friend — at least we decided that was whom he must be talking to — and those five minutes seemed ten times longer than the previous four hours. We hopped up and down on the pavement, hoping to attract the attention of the man. When he came out we allowed Harriet go in alone; we stood close to the glass with our noses pressed against it. We could just make out what she was doing in the dim light.

She put in her two pennies, dialled the number. She held the receiver against her ear. "I'm frozen," whispered Sally. "Hush," said I. We watched anxiously. She was still holding the black receiver against her ear but not speaking. She pushed the door open a fraction with her toe.

"They're not answering."

We were to discover later that they were out touring the streets and calling at every person's house that anyone could vaguely connect with us. Half of the girls in our form were dragged out of bed.

Harriet re-joined us. "You'd better try your folks, Sally. There's bound to be someone in at your house."

Sally went into the box and dialled, leaving the door slightly ajar. "Engaged," she said after a second. "Trust them!"

"Press Button B," cried Harriet, but too late, for already Sally was replacing the receiver. Our money was lost. We only had one penny left amongst us.

"You gals finished?" An American voice behind us made us jump. We let him go into the booth.

"I don't suppose we could ask to borrow a penny from him, do you?" asked Sally.

"Certainly not," said Harriet. "He might think we were trying to get off with him."

What now? We stood in a dejected huddle outside the City Hall, a long way from home. Approximately three miles to mine, four to Harriet's. We all had blisters on our heels, and we all admitted to them.

"We can't stand here all night," I said. "We'd better start walking."

"Walking?" echoed Sally.

But there was nothing else for it. We could hardly sit on the pavement waiting for a miracle to happen and we could see no one we could approach to borrow even one penny. If there had been a kindly looking woman about we might have asked her, but all the shadowy figures passing in the mist seemed to be men. We had been told that if we had to ask anyone for anything always to choose a policeman or a kindly looking woman. Our luck was out that night; we didn't catch as much as a glimpse of a member of the Royal Ulster Constabulary though we were not sure anyway that we wished to get involved with the police. They might ask a few awkward questions. It was unheard of for a policeman to ask none.

We set off. The streets stretched ahead like endless grey tunnels and we had not the heart or strength to sing now, or to talk about Hollywood. We did half-heartedly embark on *The moon at night is shining bright, Deep in the heart of Texas*, but we let it fizzle out. On a damp, moonless night in Belfast it was difficult to believe in the existence of millionaires in ten gallon hats and hordes of steers thundering across sun-baked plains.

We passed row upon row of back-to-backs all looking the same; we passed shops closed and barred; we passed schools and churches which loomed against the night sky like dark hulks where no life moved or was ever likely to. We kept close together, a little afraid of these unknown areas and their unknown inhabitants. Men were going home from the pubs, mufflered and capped against the cold. Few showed any interest in us.

Belfast had never seemed such a *long* city before.

"Just as well it's not London we have to walk through," said Harriet. "That's ten times bigger." She had been there; we had not.

"Or New York," said I.

"That goes upward," said Harriet.

But not even the thought of skyscrapers could excite us now; we only wanted to get home and go to bed. But before we would be allowed to crawl under the blankets there would be Inquisitions to face. All our parents would be worried sick, we were well aware of that, but at least the Lintons and the MacCabes would not be on their own. I thought of my mother sitting by her window, the light turned off in the room behind her, the curtain pulled back so that she could watch the street and I, too, felt sick. Unless she had gone to the MacCabes, but she was not likely to have done that.

"Come on, Sally," I said irritably, for she was lagging behind.

"Let's rest a minute. It's not going to make much difference, is it?" She took off one shoe and rubbed her foot.

"How far are we, Harriet, do you think?" I asked.

She estimated we must be about half-way.

"Half-way," groaned Sally. "I'll never make it."

At that moment a police car drew up to the kerb. We shrank back against the wall of a shop. The door of the car opened and a policeman got out. He came towards us flashing a large torch, catching us full in its beam, like cornered criminals.

"You wouldn't be the three girls we're looking for, would you? Harriet Linton, Sally MacCabe. . .?"

It was not easy trying to talk our way out of this particular escapade and I don't suppose we really did. For a few days afterwards my mother kept looking at me and shaking her head as if she knew we'd been up to something other than we'd admitted to. For of course we could not reveal what we had actually been doing. We were under pain of death, Harriet said solemnly, not to talk, even if tortured. We were full of admiration for all the men we had heard about in the war who had been captured and questioned, tortured, their lives threatened, and yet their lips remained sealed. Our lips, whilst not remaining sealed, only revealed what we wished our parents to know. Not that they went as far as torturing us although Harriet hinted that hers had stopped only just short of it.

The Lintons were the most irate. Even in the bad light of the street I could tell Mr Linton's face was purple and when he spoke to Harriet he spluttered. I imagine it wasn't very good for him, a leading lawyer, to have his daughter found wandering the streets and brought home in a police car. I could feel Harriet trembling beside me. We were all trembling a bit and my heart felt as if it had descended to somewhere in the region of my stomach. Mrs Linton was very cool. Her voice made me think of icicles.

"I think you had better get into our car now, Harriet dear, and we shall take you home. Thank you very much, officer, for all your help."

The rest of us stood outside the police station in a huddle, Sally and I, the two police officers, and Mr MacCabe.

"Come on then, you two scallywags," said Mr MacCabe, and my heart rose a bit at the word scallywags. "I'd best get you back to your mothers. They're convinced you've been sold into white slavery or kidnapped by the Gerries. No such luck!"

The three men laughed and Sally and I managed feeble grins.

My mother was at her window. I said good-night to Sally and her father and went inside.

I told my story, the one we had agreed to tell. We had felt bored after tea and fancied going downtown. Yes, I knew we were not allowed to go downtown alone after dark, and I was sorry. I must have said sorry about fifty times before going to bed.

For a moment we stayed in total silence. The fire crackled and the clock ticked. She sighed.

"Didn't you realise how worried I'd be?"

"I didn't think," I mumbled sullenly. It was a well-used response; that and 'I didn't mean to.'

"Sometimes not thinking can be a crime," said my mother, and I was to remember her words later.

So what had we done downtown? she wanted to know, and where had we gone? Oh, we'd just wandered about. I was trying to sound suitably casual. Up and down the streets? Well, sort of. She was not liking my answers. Had we spoken to any strangers? We'd asked a policeman the way, I said.

"So for four hours you just walked round and round the City Hall and it didn't even occur to you that it was time to come home?"

"The time passed quickly," I said, slumped in a chair from which I thought I would never manage to rise. I had taken off my shoes and socks and propped my feet on the fender to warm. They were both skinned and bleeding but my mother did not seem in the least bit troubled about that. War wounds, I thought, gazing at them rather than at her face.

"And you didn't go in *anywhere*? Not even a milk bar for a cup of coffee or a milk shake?"

I shook my head. I had already told her we had no money.

"Well, I fail to see how you could spend *four* hours just idling around the City Hall."

I conceded we may have wandered a little way from it.

"Oh, so you did! Where to be precise?"

We didn't know. It had been misty.

For a moment she sat contemplating the dying embers of the fire. Then she looked me straight in the face forcing me to look her in the eye. I was concealing something, she said; she did not believe I had told her the whole truth.

There was nothing more I could say. In that case I should go to bed. I was starving but did not dare ask even for a crust.

The next day she returned to her questioning but I gave no ground. She made me promise never to do anything like that again, and I did. There was no talk of punishments but she did say that she did not want me hanging around in the dark in future, and that was an order.

The MacCabes went through a bit of a shouting match and at the end of it told Sally that she was to be in at six o'clock every night. They put no time limit on their curb, such as indefinitely, or for a month, and, as Sally predicted, they forgot about it after a couple of days. But we knew we wouldn't dare repeat the outing.

Harriet fared worst. Her parents were disappointed in her, had thought they could trust her. She was not even to cross the road after dark again unaccompanied by an adult and she was not allowed to have anyone in for tea or go to anyone else's house for tea for the rest of the term.

"What a bore," she sighed, as we warmed our hands around the bunsen burner in the chemistry lab. The room was freezing except at the top where the teacher was sitting on the fireguard scorching her tweed bottom. The day was so cold that she remained on the guard for most of the lesson not daring to venture into the icy regions at the far end, which gave us peace to get on with our meeting. We were trying to decide how to proceed with our investigations with these new restrictions imposed on us. "Well, it's me mostly, isn't it?" said Harriet. She seemed to be quite proud of her parents' reactions. Of course she had come out of it all much more dramatically than we had. I began to feel my mother had let me off too lightly.

"Kate and I'll carry on, " said Sally.

"Of course," said I, jumping as my finger touched the flame.

We did not consider giving up, not now that we had made some progress and our dossiers were beginning to fill. These notebooks were top secret and we had gone so far as to write that on them, which in Sally's case would only attract her brothers to read them. I kept mine under the carpet in my bedroom when it wasn't on my person. We had taken to using phrases like that since they seemed fitting for our activities.

"You are very careful with your notebook, aren't you, Sally?" asked Harriet.

"Do you have to ask me such stupid questions, Harriet Linton?"

When the bell rang we had to go to German. Filing past the chemistry teacher, who had risen from her perch, we noticed she had scorched the back of her skirt. We left giggling and arrived in the same state in Fraulein Berg's room.

She rapped on her attaché case.

"Quiet, *bitte*. *Bitte*!"

We quietened because we liked to sit and watch her, to try to see if we could find any clues in her face or behaviour. Her face is imprinted on my mind much more clearly than that of any other teacher, even though she stayed with us for a relatively short time. Her dark eyes often looked feverish and her mouth twitched and she blinked overmuch.

"She is guilty," wrote Harriet on a piece of paper and passed it along.

"What is that you are passing, Harriet?"

"Nothing, Fraulein."

"I saw you give something to Kathleen." Today she sounded firmer, as if she had decided to take a stronger line with us.

I crumpled the paper in my fist.

"Come forward, Kathleen."

At that moment the door opened. Enter Miss Thistlethwaite. She could always be relied on to appear at the most inopportune moment, for us.

The class rose and chanted, "Good morning, Miss Thistlethwaite." She acknowledged the greeting and indicated that we should be seated. I was left standing half-way up the aisle.

"What is it, Kathleen?"

Fraulein Berg, unusual colour staining her cheeks, explained what had been happening.

"I see. Bring me whatever Harriet gave you, Kathleen."

I went forward with my hand sweating and crushing the paper. I willed it to be ground into pulp. I considered putting it into my mouth and swallowing hard but every eye was upon me, not least the headmistress's. I had to hold out the squashed piece of greyish paper.

She straightened it out and peered through the bottom half of her spectacles, the reading part. She frowned.

"She is guilty," she read in a loud voice. "To whom does this refer, Harriet?"

Harriet stood. "No one, Miss Thistlethwaite."

"Then why write it?"

"It was just a joke."

"A joke? Can you explain it then so that we may all share it? We all like jokes. Don't we, girls?"

Everyone was looking at Harriet and the headmistress; I stole a quick glance at the German teacher. Her face was quite pale; all the colour had left it.

Harriet, scarlet-faced, was saying that she couldn't really explain it, but she was not going to be let off the hook as lightly as that. Miss Thistlethwaite was known for her persistence and tenacity. It must be possible to explain a joke, she insisted. And who was the *she* referred to? And what was *she* guilty of? She hissed on the 'shes' and spittle flecked her lips.

"Nothing."

"So *she* is *not* guilty then?"

"No."

"You must make up your mind, Harriet."

I was beginning to think we might pass the rest of the period in this way. Miss Thistlethwaite loved such games. There were times when we didn't know what she was talking about by the time she finished and certainly couldn't remember the point at which she had begun. Today we could not forget the point as she waved the grey crumpled paper to and fro like a miniature rag to remind us. She stopped giving Harriet the third degree and delivered to us all instead a lecture on paying attention and not wasting the teacher's valuable time. And of course we knew that it was totally forbidden to write notes to one another in class. What would it be like if we were all to sit writing notes? She gave Harriet a hundred lines for writing this particular note and fifty to me for receiving it. I had been an accomplice: I had had the

71

freedom to refuse or accept.

"You must always recognise your responsibilities, girls. You are free to choose between good and evil."

'I must not write notes in class, especially when they are jokes that have no meaning,' Harriet had to write one hundred times.

'I must not accept passed notes in class,' I had to write fifty times.

"I think now, Harriet, you might remove yourself to the cloakroom and ponder a while on what I have said."

We had no doubt but that she would sit on the bench where we changed our Wellies and begin on the writing of her lines.

By the time Miss Thistlethwaite took herself off, the period was almost over. We just had time to finish learning the present tense of the verb *sehen*, to see.

"*Ich sehe dich*," cried Harriet, jumping out on us from behind a row of damp coats in the cloakroom as we came in.

"*Wir sehen Fraulein Berg*," chanted Sally and I.

That afternoon the two of us did what we could to see Fraulein Berg. Harriet had an elocution lesson.

"How now brown cow," said Sally in an affected Oxford voice, as we loitered around the grocer's window pretending to take an interest in his display of Heinz baked beans.

Fraulein Berg had bought a pound of broken biscuits and two ounces of Cheddar cheese and disappeared into her flat. So far her head had not appeared at the window.

"There she is," I said, whirling round.

Sally turned too and as we gazed up she looked down and saw us.

"*Sie sieht uns*," said Sally.

"*Jawohl*," said I.

We turned back to contemplate the beans.

I confessed that I had a feeling that Fraulein Berg had seen me before when I had been hanging around spying on her.

Sally nodded. She felt the same. So she must suspect that we were watching her. Sally thought she might go and complain to the headmistress but I didn't. For what could she say? "Every time I turn around I see these girls watching me"?

We decided to give up for the afternoon. Our feet felt like chunks of ice anyway, and we were hungry. Sally came home with me and I made some hot cocoa which we drank in our little kitchenette looking out on to the back yard. The washing hung stiff as a board from the taut line. The damp had given way to frost with the dwindling of the day. We talked about Fraulein Berg. Perhaps we should ease off for a day or two so that she would think we had given up and then she might relax her guard. If she had one up.

The following afternoon as we came out of school we saw that she was on the hill in front of us. But she was not alone. Beside her, pushing his bicycle, walked Mr McGuffie, our music teacher, the only male teacher in the school. He was about fifty years old and almost completely bald, except for a few tufts of gingerish-fair hair that stuck up around the edges of his ears. He was a widower.

They were talking, heads turned inward to one another, he with his hands placed square on the handlebars of his bicycle, she holding hers primly before her carrying the attaché case.

"Don't tell me he fancies her," said Harriet with disgust.

"Don't tell me she fancies *him*," said I.

Which made us feel that perhaps they might fancy one another, since no one else might. We followed with interest, keeping a suitable distance between us and them, not stopping even to go into our ice cream shop. They were moving slowly and talking with animation. Her laugh rang out in the clear air. It was a sharp frosty day without a touch of damp. Unusual for Belfast where the streets stay wet much of the year. What could they be talking about?

"Mr McGuffie could hardly be a spy too, could he?" said Sally dubiously.

A spy, Mr McGuffie? It was hard to imagine. We had always found him to be one of our most boring teachers, and with a crowd like ours to choose from that was saying something. "Now then, girls, let me hear that high Doh." We nicknamed him High Doh. He frequently got himself worked up to that pitch. We chattered and ate sweets in his class and sang off-key deliberately and generally drove him mad. Presumably he was unable to obtain employment at a more desirable establishment. For a while Harriet had gone to him for piano lessons but she said he had put his arm round her waist and her parents removed her to send her to a better teacher. Not because of his arm — she didn't tell them about that — but because she wasn't learning anything. A born loser, poor Mr McGuffie.

"I know," said Harriet suddenly. "He's in the Home Guard."

We looked at her.

"He could be useful to her. Well, of course, he could, he would know where the secret dug-outs are and so forth."

What secret dug-outs? we wanted to know, feeling again enormously uninformed. Harriet said that there were secret hide-outs where all the important people would go in case of invasion, and from these places they would rule the country. We presumed Mr Linton would be amongst them.

"Do they think we're going to be invaded?" asked Sally. At the beginning of the war we had been waiting for it, expecting to see a column of steel-helmeted Germans with batons at the ready coming across the border any day. It would be their obvious way in, according to Mr MacCabe, but my mother said they would then have the Irish Sea to cross and she was sure that would have occurred to the Germans too. They might be daft but they weren't that daft. And, anyway, she seemed to think we had passed the point of invasion; if they'd been going to come they'd have come in 1940. Mr MacCabe said it was a mistake to be complacent where the Enemy was concerned. By Enemy he meant Germans, IRA, the Republic of Ireland; and after the war the Russians were included. Even during the war he kept shaking his head and saying he wasn't too sure about those Reds and Britain would rue the day she'd taken them on as allies.

We looked at the back view of the music teacher. His legs were gripped round the ankles by bicycle clips and his long grubby trench coat swirled just above them, dipping at the side as he leant over his ancient rusty bicycle. It was a ladies' bicycle, upright, with a basket fastened to the front handlebars. He didn't look as if he would be possession of a secret to anything. One could never tell of course. We remembered a girl in our class who was always sweet and goody-goody, a darling of the teachers, who would trust her with their last sticks of chalk — the chalk was severely rationed out — and she had been caught stealing from the teachers' cloakroom. The teachers', not even the pupils'!

"You could be right, Harriet," I said slowly.

When they reached the shops they stopped and he propped his bicycle against his right leg as if he meant to stand for a while. We had to pass them. We said, "Good afternoon," in our best voices, and High Doh said in a hearty voice, "Good afternoon, girls." He seemed in good fettle. We were of the opinion that Fraulein Berg blushed.

Harriet left us (it was ballet day) and Sally and I went into Mr Dyson's for some cinnamon bark. They were still standing there when we came out sucking it.

"Let's go in and see my dad."

Mr MacCabe was cutting chops. Whack! went his chopper as it came down on the chopping board. We sucked our cinnamon and he cut his chops and across the road the pair of them chatted and laughed.

"What've you two been up to today then?"

"Nothing." We peered round the carcass of a pig. They were moving. Fraulein Berg was detaching herself to go into the grocer's, High Doh was waiting by the kerb, twisting his hands round and round on the handlebars. Surely she was not going to ask him up to tea!

"What's so interesting?" Mr MacCabe left his counter and came to stand beside us, cleaver in his blood-stained hand. I would hate to be a butcher, I thought, shuddering at the sight of the blade. When I was small my mother could never persuade me to walk on the blood-stained sawdust floor. It was only when I met Sally that I got over my distaste of butchers' shops. Not that I ever got to like them but I did learn to tolerate them.

Fraulein Berg was emerging clutching her bag of biscuits. They waited at the kerb, he looking right and left, allowing a bus and two cars to pass, then he nodded, indicating that they should go. She scuttled across the road beside him and his bicycle and they were gone from our sight.

"Place looks like it always does," remarked Mr MacCabe.

We left him to his chopping and nipped over to the haberdashery window. Mrs McCurdy had some new wool in, some pretty greens and pinks. We studied it for a moment before turning to look back and up. Her lamp was lit and we could see two heads, his and hers. Downstairs, outside the door of her flat, stood his bicycle, its rear wheel bound to its chain with an enormous heavy link chain. He was a cautious man, Mr McGuffie, usually.

"Daisy, Daisy," sang Sally, "give me your answer do."

Sally and I walked home pondering on this new development, getting from it every ounce of interest that could be extracted. Give us a molehill and we could raise a mountain within minutes.

Mrs Linton was in my mother's room having a fitting. I heard her voice as I let myself in so after I had dropped my school bag in the hall I took my library books from my room and scuttled off to the library to change them. Our nearest library was a fair walk, getting on for a mile, and it was nothing special when you did get there, but it was better than nothing. Once it had been an ordinary shop but the windows had been painted over to blot them out and the inside fitted with shelves. The stock was so limited that I was in danger of running through it before the war would be over. When the war ended — everything was going to happen then! — we would get new books and a new library and all the old ones would be thrown into the rubbish bucket where they belonged. They stank, quite a number of them, and my mother said I should be selective, meaning that I should choose my books for their condition as well as their content. The trouble was that the popular ones were the dirtiest and tended to be splotched with lumps of egg (dried and reconstituted probably), and coffee and tea stains. You could see what all the previous readers had been having for their teas and breakfasts. I was not allowed to read at the table and was astonished that so many mothers let their children eat and read at the same time. I envied them.

The lights were on inside the library and in spite of the vague smell and the hemmed-in space I enjoyed browsing around. I was crazy about books and could never get enough to read. I had read every Enid Blyton book I could lay my hands on, every Chalet School story, Just William, Biggles, Worrals, L.M. Montgomery, Angela Brazil, Louisa M Alcott, and dozens of others. The first title my eye lit on today was *School Versus Spy* which I seized eagerly, and then I saw *Schoolgirls in Peril*. The second one was set in Occupied France. I hugged them to my chest as I ran all the way home and in the evening, once I had done my latin homework, I read them both, finishing the second with the light of a torch beneath the blankets. I could never sleep with a book unfinished. When I did sleep I dreamt of spies, and in my

77

dream I saw Fraulein Berg chasing Mr McGuffie through a misty landscape that I somehow knew was Occupied France.

"Run!" I was shouting.

I wakened my mother who came in to soothe me from my nightmare. She said in the morning that I looked like death warmed up and I shouldn't read books about spies if they were going to give me nightmares. Apparently I had been muttering about spies in my sleep before I had shouted to High Doh to run.

We met going down the road to school that morning, Sally and Harriet and I, and High Doh passed us trilling his bicycle bell merrily and calling out that it was a lovely morning.

"I'm half crazy," sang Sally, "all for the love of you."

Harriet frowned. "Perhaps we should warn him. About Fraulein Berg."

We did not see how we were going to do that. Of course Harriet was very confident when it came to talking, due to the influence of her father the lawyer and all those elocution lessons, but we thought it might be too tricky a situation for even her to handle. How could she say, 'Beware of Fraulein Berg!'? It was not necessary to *say* anything, she replied, we could write him a message.

"And sign it?" I asked.

She thought that would be unwise.

I said I thought it was supposed to be a terrible crime to send anonymous letters.

"Oh, Kate, you are an idiot! Only if they are nasty letters. We will watch what we say though, just in case." Did she mean in case we were found out? She pursed her lips and would not be specific. We would not mention Fraulein Berg by name. By the time we reached the school gate we had a message composed in our heads.

It would be too dangerous to write it in school so after the last bell we went in the opposite direction from our homes to the next group of shops where we were not known. We bought a pad of plain white paper and one envelope. Nearby was a chip shop in which you could sit and eat chips or drink coca cola. We bought a glass of coca cola and three straws and sat in one of the horse boxes.

"You write, Kate," said Harriet. "Yours is the best writing."

Flattery often does get people somewhere. I, in my vanity, was pleased to wield the pen. I printed in my best block capitals the following message:

'Take care with whom you associate. Your country relies on you.' I signed it 'A well wisher.'

I folded the sheet of paper and put it in its envelope, then carefully printed his address. We knew where he lived since one day, out of idleness, we had followed him home. It sounds as though we spent a large part of our time following people but, until the Fraulein came into our lives, it had only been a very occasional event and usually because we had nothing else to do.

Harriet had a stamp which had been delivered unfranked on a letter and she had steamed off. She had foreseen the need for glue too, had a tube in her pocket. She was always well prepared, we had to hand it to her. She affixed the stamp with a resounding smack of her fist which made the man behind the counter look up from the football coupon which he was filling in. Sally's father did the pools regularly every week, the house had to be semi-peaceful on a Thursday evening so that he could concentrate as the form had to be in the post first thing Friday morning. Once he had won a hundred pounds and the MacCabes had had the biggest party the neighbourhood had ever known. For a week or two after that we filled in a coupon, Harriet and Sally and I, and paid Mr MacCabe sixpence to send it in for us, but we had no luck. You had to persevere, said Mr MacCabe, in all walks of life.

We took our letter two pillar boxes further downtown. You couldn't be too careful when it came to covering your tracks: we knew that. Sally committed it to the gaping mouth of the red box and as I watched it slide irretrievably inward I felt a terrible weight of guilt descend upon me. Without doubt I would have been dead useless as a Resistance fighter. I was relieved that I had not had the ill luck to find myself behind the German lines after the outbreak of war.

On Friday evening my mother took me to the cinema. We arrived just as the organist, playing *Lili Marlene*, was coming up out of the floor. My mother quite enjoyed the musical recital but I was not completely absorbed by it so I did a reconnaissance to see who else was in the audience. Two rows behind, with a girl, sat Tommy MacCabe, Sally's oldest brother. I twisted my neck round as far as it would go but failed to see who the girl was because of a woman with a large head sitting in front of her.

"Sit still," whispered my mother.

Obediently, I put my hands in my lap but only for a moment for then I caught sight of Fraulein Berg sitting straight ahead of us, about three rows down. She was with Mr McGuffie!

"Sit still," said my mother again. I had kicked her on the ankle in my excitement.

I forgot about them during the film — it would have taken a lot to distract me from a good going Western — but as soon as the lights went up at the interval I remembered them at once. He was getting up, easing himself past the other people in the row, his bald head nodding as he asked each one to excuse him. Then he went up the aisle to where the ice cream and cigarette girl stood with her tray. He bought two ice creams and carried them back to his companion in triumph.

"You are a fidget tonight," said my mother.

After the second film, the main feature, we stood to sing *God Save the King*. Half of the people in the cinema were busy trying to exit but my mother always insisted that we stand still and sing our national anthem. She said it was terribly undignified to cut and run like that as if you couldn't spare a minute for the poor King. The war must be a terrible burden for him. As the rows in front cleared I saw that my two teachers were still standing. I could hear Mr McGuffie's voice — being a musician he could sing fairly well — rising clearly above everyone else's. He sounded quite carried away, especially when he got to the line 'Happy and Glorious'; his shoulders were straight and his head was flung back. Was Fraulein Berg singing? I could not hear her voice but did not expect to alongside his and from the back view of her head I could not decide. I wondered how I would like to have to stand up for *Deutschland über Alles*.

The last chord crashed and died away. I scrambled under the seat for my dropped gloves.

"Want to go up for an ice cream?" asked my mother, smiling.

The café was crowded by the time we got up there — one reason why people raced out before the anthem was sung. We were lucky to find an empty table hidden behind a pillar and a potted plant.

The waitresses were scurrying about with harassed frowns knotting their brows and getting quite worked up if anyone called, 'Miss!' after them too insistently. My mother and I sat and waited patiently, not minding about the wait as it was part of our treat to sit and watch the rest of the people. Since it was our neighbourhood cinema we always saw somebody we knew, or at least I did, and then I would give my mother the run down on them. I was out and about more than she was, obviously.

I was peering round the pillar when I saw my two teachers entering the café. They must have been the last to leave the auditorium. I could imagine him standing ramrod-still until the last suspicion of a note died away from *God Save the King*. If he was that patriotic it was a bit odd him keeping company with a German. Unless he was a counter spy of course, detailed to keep an eye on *her*. An interesting possibility.

He was leading the way, moving in and out between the crowded tables, peering short-sightedly to see if there were any vacant spaces. I shrank back behind the pillar and tried to make myself thin.

"Are you having an ice cream then?" asked my mother.

The waitress was beside us, pencil and pad in hand. We gave our order. I felt overshadowed on my left hand side and looked up to see Mr McGuffie regarding the two empty seats at our table covetously.

"Are these free?" he asked my mother.

She nodded and said that they were and it was only as he ushered the Fraulein into a seat that he turned and recognised me.

"Ah, Kathleen!"

I was embarrassed but so were they. I had to introduce them to my mother and immediately Mr McGuffie engaged her in conversation, about me. My face must have been the colour of the tomato sauce bottle on the table. He was telling her what a marvellous ear I had and what a pity it was I didn't have piano lessons.

"I would be very happy to take her on as a pupil, Mrs Carson."

My mother said that was kind of him but we didn't have a piano. His face dropped but only momentarily. He was a bouyant man; a blow only served to make him come back

83

more forcibly. He was sure that little problem could be overcome, he declared.

"What do you say, Hildegarde?"

Hildegarde looked as if she did not wish to say anything. She had been sitting as quiet as a mouse with her hands in her lap. My mother saved her the necessity of voicing an opinion by coming in to say that we would think about it.

"Do!" urged Mr McGuffie. "A natural talent, I feel sure of it." (He was desperate for pupils since none stayed with him more than a term.) "She is a very clever girl, you know, your daughter."

I eyed the waitress who had emerged from the swing door at the back with a laden tray but she went straight past us. When she returned on her homeward run, High Doh snapped his fingers and called out, "Miss!" but she didn't even bat an eyelid. She edged her hip against the swing door and disappeared from our sight.

"The service is very poor here," sighed my mother.

"Perhaps we should not wait?" ventured Fraulein Berg, unheard by her companion. He was getting ready for the waitress's next appearance. He had his fingers held at the ready. She came out and veered off in a different direction.

We all looked at one another and looked away, (my mother and Fraulein Berg exchanging half-smiles) except for High Doh who regarded each one of us full in the face in turn. He seemed much more sure of himself than I had ever seen him. He seemed in high spirits. Wait till he got his post in the morning! I wondered if he would be as snappy and talkative then. Whilst he waited for the waitress to come within hailing distance he began to discuss the film, addressing most of his remarks to my mother. Hildegarde and I stayed silent gazing at the white tablecloth. Not even a Knickerbocker Glory would be worth the agony of all this. I had never had one of those sumptuous ice creams but Sally had, on her trips to Dublin, and had described them to me in full detail until I had had to cry, "Stop!" She was still talking about me going with them at half-term but I hadn't even mentioned it to my mother. We'd just had gas and electricity bills in and she had been hard pushed to pay them.

At last the waitress stopped at our table. She set down a cup of coffee and a vanilla ice cream topped with raspberry sauce. Normally I would have picked up my spoon and eaten slowly, relishing each mouthful, but tonight I wanted to gobble it down as fast as possible and get out of the place. During the last few minutes I thought I could feel Fraulein Berg's downcast eyes somehow watching from under those heavy, lowered lids. I sensed a feeling of unease coming from her, difficult to explain; I only knew that she made me feel uncomfortable.

High Doh gave his order and sat back and smiled as if he had won a major victory. My mother drank her coffee. I spooned up my ice cream scraping the last droplet from the silver bowl. I glanced at my mother and was relieved to see she was picking her handbag up from the floor. We said good-night and left.

I saw him only ten hours later. I was doing the shopping round for my mother, going from the butcher to the baker to the grocer, when I saw him crossing the main road and going into the police station. My basket dropped with a thud at my feet. In a panic I lifted it and took the two eggs from their bag, feeling all round their smooth surfaces for any sign of a crack. My mother would have a fit if I had damaged our precious egg ration. There was the teeniest sliver of a crack on one which, with any luck, she wouldn't notice.

I could return my attention now to High Doh. What *was* he doing inside the police station? My heart was hammering. It was hardly likely that he had caught sight of any of the men in the *Wanted* ads outside. We always studied their faces going past — they looked grim and criminal-like — and afterwards scanned every face we passed in the street hoping we might recognise one and be able to claim the reward. They were mostly members of the I.R.A., according to Harriet.

Perhaps Mr McGuffie had gone into the police station to give a report on Fraulein Berg. But I could not really talk myself into believing that one, not with her living only a few yards down the street. There was only one reason I could think of for his visit and the thought of that made me feel sick. The note was in my writing. I had just had a tuppenny bar of milk chocolate, my Saturday morning treat, and now it was sitting uneasily on my stomach.

He came out of the station and I almost dropped the basket again. He didn't notice me. He was frowning and thinking of something else other than Saturday morning shoppers. He barged through them, dodged a woman with a pram and a child on a tricycle, then stopped on the kerb before sprinting across the road. I had a fairly good idea of where he might be going.

He scratched the top of his bald head whilst he waited for the door to be opened and the moment that it did, he bolted inside and I didn't even get a glimpse of her.

"Are you stuck to the spot then, Kate?" I jumped. Billy MacCabe had come out of his father's shop and was grinning at me like an idiot. He had Danny Forbes with him. "You've been standing there for about three hours."

"Where's Harriet the day?" asked Danny.

"Harriet's handy with the lariat," said Billy and doubled up with amusement at himself.

I tossed my head at them — really, they were insufferably boring! — and sauntered off down the street to continue my shopping, taking care to keep an eye on Fraulein Berg's door, which meant that I had a crick in my neck by the time I emerged from the grocer's with a full basket. Outside, I met a girl who had been in my class at elementary school and we had a bit of a crack together. I wiggled round her until she had her back to the street and I my face to the road. Every now and then I had to break off and say hello to other passers-by. The whole world seemed to be out on a Saturday morning. Of Harriet there was no sign for her mother got her shopping delivered, and Sally had gone downtown with her mother to buy a new dress for going to Dublin. They had been saving up their coupons, said Mrs MacCabe, but I knew fine well that they would be going to a shop whose owner Mr MacCabe supplied with meat. I had a feeling Mrs MacCabe hadn't meant me to take her seriously anyway. She had a twinkle in her eye.

Eventually, the other girl said she'd better be off, her mother was waiting for the meat to cook the dinner. As I was about to move along too I heard another voice greeting me, one that it did not cheer me up to hear.

"Good morning, Kathleen."

I turned. The headmistress with her dog on a short lead stood before me.

"Good morning, Miss Thistlethwaite," I chanted, as we did in class.

The dog snapped at me and jumped towards my basket. Miss Thistlethwaite jerked his rein and said soothingly, "Now, Benny, be a good boy. The basket belongs to Kathleen." She smiled and stooped to pat his head. He was a horrible little dog, we all hated him at school; every time we passed he barked and snapped and his owner had a habit of looking at us as if it was our fault.

As Miss Thistlethwaite lifted her head her face changed. She had seen something not to her liking across the road. I whirled round. Mr McGuffie was being let out of the door by Fraulein Berg. The headmistress was frowning, pursing her lips until the bottom one stuck out almost like a saucer. I wondered if I could get my mouth into that shape but decided that was not the moment to try. The dog barked again and reared up on his hind legs.

"Down, Benny, down," she said absentmindedly.

Mr McGuffie was saying a few last words to Fraulein Berg. She nodded, smiled, and then he backed away bumping into a woman laden with shopping baskets in both hands. She gave him a tongueful: we could tell without hearing. A bus passed.

"Come, Benny, come! Good day, Kathleen."

"Good day, Miss Thistlethwaite."

Headmistress and dog crossed the street, she walking briskly in her pointed-toe, buttoned shoes, he dancing with little steps and yap, yap, yapping, as if he was going off on a rabbit hunt. They soon caught up with High Doh. I watched them continue down the street together. She was doing all the talking.

That time at the door was the last occasion on which I saw Mr McGuffie alone with Fraulein Berg. After that they passed in the corridors and exchanged nods and at morning prayers she did not look anywhere near the piano. Sally and Harriet thought it was because of our letter warning him off but I was not so sure. And now I am pretty certain that it was Miss Thistlethwaite who brought that relationship to an end. I can imagine what she might have said to him. "In our profession we cannot be too careful, Mr McGuffie, we must set an example for our girls. It would not do for us to become talking points, subjects of rumour and even scandal." And he, being the only man we were subjected to at school, must be extra careful. No doubt too she would have dropped hints questioning the desirability of keeping him on in a girls' school and I suppose he would have been worried about getting another job. According to Harriet, he was not properly qualified, had no letters after his name.

And so that budding romance came to an end. Fraulein Berg looked sad for a few days and after that seemed much as before.

"She couldn't have been in *love* with him, after all," said Sally. "So she's not going to pine away from a broken heart."

She went back to walking up the road after school alone, buying her broken biscuits and one or two other groceries, and then going up to her room to light the lamp and have her cup of tea. We got bored staring at the outline of her head against the lamplight so when we saw her settled in her chair we usually went home.

The following Saturday I went to Sally's for tea. Harriet was not allowed to come of course although she did ask again in the hopes that they might relent, but they didn't. Mrs MacCabe was baking when I arrived at the back door. I always went to the back, knocked and poked my head round. The door was never locked. The smells were delicious. Mrs MacCabe had a couple of fruit tarts cooling on the rack, a pile of scones gathered in a tea towel, and she was mixing up cake batter. Sally and I got the bowl to scrape.

"I've been wondering, Kate," said Mrs MacCabe, as she closed the oven door and wiped her hands down her apron, "if you'd like to come to Dublin with Sally and me? It'd be my treat."

"Oh, but I couldn't —"

"Sure, why not? It's Sally's birthday that week-end and she'd love to have you for company. I'll have my sister Nell with me, you see, and Sally gets right bored trailing round the shops after us, don't you, love?"

Sally, her mouth full of batter, nodded. I put down my spoon and locked my hands in a vice-like grip. It seemed too good to be true and I wasn't prepared to believe that it could happen yet. I knew what my mother was going to say. She was proud and didn't like to accept charity.

"I'll have a word with your mother. I'd take Harriet as well but I don't suppose her parents would let her go, do you?"

"You could ask," said Sally, her mouth now clear. "It'd be good if the three of us could be together for my birthday."

"It would be fantastic," said I.

We were restless now with thoughts of Dublin swirling in our heads. We went up to the shops and bought some liquorice root and loitered around on the pavement eyeing Fraulein Berg's flat. She seemed either to be out or in bed for there was not a sign of life at the sitting room window.

"Let's go up the Antrim Road and scout around that house again," said Sally. "We can get back before tea and it's not as if it's dark or anything."

Before jumping on a bus we checked our money this time. We had both got our pocket money that morning so we had sufficient to cover the fares all the way there *and* back. We enjoyed the ride into town and up the Antrim Road. The sun was shining and we sat on the front seat of the top deck. Belfast didn't seem such a bad old place with the sun on it. It might not come up to Hollywood standards but you couldn't expect that. Hollywood was in a class all of its own.

We were not sure if we would remember which stop to get off at and didn't, not until we had passed it; so we had to walk back, but only a few hundred yards so we didn't mind. And we found the street quite easily since we had the address written in our notebooks. It looked different in daylight, innocent and ordinary. One man was digging in his front garden doing his bit for the 'Dig for Victory' campaign. Since the war started people didn't grow flowers so much and it was quite common to see potatoes and other vegetables growing in a front garden. The night that we had come here I had felt the street to be a place of shadows and secrets.

We slowed our steps as we approached number twenty-seven. Of course we hadn't thought out what we planned to do and we didn't have Harriet here to tell us.

"We could knock at the door and ask if somebody or other lives here," suggested Sally.

"We could," I agreed. Who would do the asking? I had written the anonymous letter.

"O.K.," said Sally, "I'll do it."

90

As we went up the short drive, our feet scrunched on the gravel making what I felt to be a terrible noise and I expected a face to appear at the bay window any minute. None did. Sally stepped up into the porch and rang the bell. I glanced down the street but no one seemed interested in us. The man in the garden was still bent over his spade.

The door opened and a dark-haired woman appeared on the step.

"Yes?" Although she only said that one word we knew she was not British.

For a second I thought Sally would fall off the step but she recovered balance and found her voice. "Do the Lintons live here, please, by any chance?"

"Lintons?"

"Yes. Mr and Mrs. And there is a daughter Harriet about the same age as us." Sally had started to gabble now.

Then I looked beyond her and the woman at the door and saw that another figure had come into the hall. She came forward and the light fell on her face. It was Fraulein Berg.

We didn't get a proper hold of ourselves until we were back in the middle of the city and well clear of the Antrim Road. Once we had put a distance between us and Fraulein Berg we were able to collapse into a state of giggling. We stood outside the City Hall and laughed until our stomachs ached. A flower seller, no doubt irritated by the inane noise, got up and shook the water from a bunch of early daffodils on to our feet.

"Lovely fresh daffs," she cried, giving us a filthy look.

We edged away and she returned to sit in the centre of her ring of flower buckets.

We hadn't felt like laughing when we saw Fraulein Berg appearing in the hallway. She came right forward to join her friend on the doorstep. She did not smile.

"Sally?" she said sharply. "And Kathleen? What are you doing here?"

Her friend spoke to her in German. Sally and I backed away a step or two but did not dare retreat further for her eye was fixed upon us.

"So, you are looking for some people?"

"Lintons," said the other woman.

"It doesn't matter," said Sally.

"Wait!" Fraulein Berg held up her hand. "You surely cannot mean Harriet Linton?"

"Yes, yes, that is what they said," put in her friend. "Harriet Linton."

"You know perfectly well where Harriet Linton lives."

"It wasn't Harriet exactly," faltered Sally.

"It's her cousin we're looking for," I said. "She lives somewhere round here. . . Harriet told us." I glanced over my shoulder as if I expected to see the cousin popping up from behind the hedge.

"Really? And what is the cousin's name?"

I felt something must be stuck at the back of my throat. Sally was waiting for me to answer. I swallowed. "Heather."

Talk about getting in deeper and deeper once you start to lie! I had visions of us inventing a whole family, having to give the father and mother's Christian names and describe them in full detail.

"So you have come all this way to visit a cousin of Harriet's without knowing exactly where she lives?" Fraulein Berg gave us a long look that was so searching I was sure she could see into the bottom of my soul. If I had a soul, that was.

"A minute," said the other woman. "Perhaps Deirdre will know. Deirdre!" she called into the house.

Sally and I would have been extremely happy to have had open under us one of those animal traps they set in woods where the earth suddenly gives way and you drop downward out of sight. Of course, if we'd been in Hollywood, Errol Flynn would have come dashing up the path with his sword at the ready to rescue us. Or Johnny Weissmuller might have appeared swinging from the branches of the tree in the next door garden. There was no sign of Errol Flynn or Tarzan. Only Fraulein Berg. We did not dare to cut and run, much as we were tempted to. It was amazing that she who had virtually no influence over us in the classroom suddenly had us under her control. In her power.

Her friend returned with Deirdre whom we gathered owned the house. The German woman appeared to be her lodger.

"Linton?" said Deidre. "I can't think of anyone round here of that name. Maybe Sean would know. Sean!" she called.

Sean came in carpet slippers, with his spectacles pushed up above his hairline. He was carrying a newspaper.

"Linton?" he said. "Isn't there a fellow called Linton lives two streets over? Or is it Linley?" He scratched his ear which looked very red. I imagined he had been sitting by the fire.

"It doesn't matter," I said desperately.

"But it's a pity if you can't find your friends," said Deirdre. "Do you want to come in and look up the phone book?"

"They're not on the phone," said Sally.

"No, I imagine they are not," said Fraulein Berg.

She released us.

We had been like flies caught in a spider's web, we decided, as we waited in the bus queue at the City Hall. She had a strange power in her eyes. She might well have been trained to hypnotise people, Sally thought; that would be a useful trick for a spy to know.

"Just think she could have everybody doing what *she* wanted."

"She could make people give up information even when they didn't mean to."

"Like Mr McGuffie."

We reckoned he had had a narrow escape, even though he didn't know it.

By the time we got on a bus — they were packed on a Saturday afternoon — and arrived back at Sally's we were starving. The table was laid and everything was ready.

"By the way, Kate," said Mrs MacCabe, as she carried in the enormous big brown teapot, "I went round and had a word with your mother this afternoon. About Dublin."

I held my breath.

"She said she'd think about it."

So she hadn't said no outright! Maybe there was just a sliver of a chance I could talk her into it; or that Mrs MacCabe had, for Sally's mother was great at talking people into things.

"I told her she'd be doing me a favour. That you'd be keeping Sally from under my feet. Come on then, youse lot! Your tea's waiting on you."

She didn't need to repeat her invitation.

After we'd helped wash up, Sally and I went to her room and planned our wardrobes for the Dublin trip. I wondered if my mother might run me up a new dress. She had a lovely piece of blue woollen material lying in the drawer. And then for a moment I sobered.

"She might not let me go at all, Sally, you know."

"Ach, sure she will. Tell her my Da's got pots of dough, doesn't know what to do with it." Sally laughed.

My mother wouldn't have wanted to take money from a millionaire.

She was listening to the wireless when I came in — Saturday Night Theatre — but she didn't like the play very much so she switched it off. I had to bring up Dublin straightaway.

"Well, I don't know, love. . ."

"*Please*, Mum! They really do want me to go." And I wanted it. But I didn't have to add that.

She smiled. "You don't get too many treats, do you?" I wouldn't have agreed but, anyway, there was no point in disputing that, not at this particular moment when she looked about to crumble. "All right then, you can go!"

I almost strangled her with a hug.

She would give me my own money to spend, she said; I was not to let Mrs MacCabe pay for everything for me. She would have to pay the hotel bill for my mother could not but Mrs MacCabe said I would be sharing a room with Sally

95

anyway so it wouldn't make much difference.

I was so thrilled I couldn't sleep that night. To actually go to Dublin, to leave Northern Ireland for the first time ever! And to stay in a real hotel!

My mother and I had gone to Portrush once and stayed in a guest house, a funny wee house that could only take three families. The lobby had smelt of over-boiled greens and the tablecloths had been spotted with gravy and tomato sauce stains. My mother had said never again! Walking along the promenade one day we'd met some people from further down our street in Belfast and got into conversation. They were terribly stuck-up though they'd no cause to be and they liked to swank it over everyone else and brag about what they'd got in their house and all the different places they went to. They threw money round like water but weren't at all like the MacCabes who just liked to enjoy themselves and didn't care what anyone else had. My mother hated them. They asked us where we were staying and she kind of nodded her head in a vague direction indicating over there. (They were staying in one of the best hotels, naturally.) "Oh, the Northern Counties?" they said, and my mother did not deny it. They kept on walking with us and eventually I realised we were going in the direction of the Northern Counties, the poshest hotel in Portrush. It was almost lunch-time. "We'll just leave you to your hotel," they said. I kept my eyes on my feet. I was wearing plimsolls and they were beginning to split across the front. Every time I looked at them after the holiday, I remembered that walk through Portrush. I was glad when my mother said they were done and I could put them in the dustbin. We had to walk up the steps of the hotel to the main entrance. We looked back to wave. They waved and moved away. My mother said not a word. I wondered if she intended to walk right in. She did.

Inside she stopped. She asked the doorman a question — I was in such a state of inner turmoil I didn't know what —

96

then she turned and we walked out again. At the foot of the steps she took off her shoe and upended it. No stone fell out.

The coast was clear. Hastily we made our way back to our boarding house.

"Horrible people," she said.

We never mentioned the incident again and when we saw them coming another day we nipped smartly round a corner.

In Dublin the hotel would not smell of boiled cabbage and Brussel sprouts and they would never let stains lie on their tablecloths for a second. They would be whipped off at once and the head waiter would snap his fingers for a new one to be brought.

Harriet groaned with envy when she heard the news.

"You can come too if they'd let you," said Sally.

"We'll see," said Harriet.

We didn't have much hope that she would be allowed to, but as Sally said, one never knew with Harriet. She was used to getting her own way, was clever at it.

On Monday afternoon we had to face Fraulein Berg. Sally said she was feeling sick and she wondered if we couldn't both go to Matron and ask to lie down in the Sick Room. I didn't think we'd get away with that.

"We'll have to face her sometime."

"I suppose you're right."

Harriet was well primed and if Fraulein Berg was to quiz her she knew what the answers were to be. Yes, she had a cousin called Heather and they used to live up the Antrim Road, but now had moved to Malone. She didn't have to give any answers for the Fraulein did not enquire about her relations. She said nothing to Sally and me about anything other than matters arising out of our German lesson. Her gaze, when it rested on us, was distinctly cool. We waited till she was well up the hill after school and did not hang around outside the grocer's watching for her head to appear at the window.

There were only two weeks to go until half-term. My mother cut out a dress for me in the blue material and I took a piece of the spare cloth up to the haberdasher's to buy a length of satin ribbon to match it for an Alice band. I told Mrs McCurdy all about the forthcoming week-end and she leant on the counter and said wasn't I the lucky one? It was many a long day since she'd set foot in Dublin but she used to enjoy a trip to the city when her husband was alive. "He used to enjoy a good fling, God rest his soul! It's real nice of the MacCabes to take you, so it is. Of course they're dead generous. You might wonder where some of his money comes from but at least he doesn't hug it tight to his own chest."

The door jingled open and in came Mrs Linton in her fur coat with its fox's tippet for a collar. I hated the sight of that dead fox lying around her neck. Sally said it was real fashionable but I would never care enough about fashion to want to wear dead animal heads slung about my neck.

I paid for my ribbon and Mrs McCurdy slipped it into a little bag.

"Kate's going to Dublin with the MacCabes," she said.

"Isn't that nice?" Mrs Linton smiled, giving nothing away.

Next day at school Harriet was a bit dejected. "They say they don't think so." To me she said, "Now if it had been your mother — "

My mother finished my dress and it was beautiful. It fitted snugly round my wrists and nipped me in at the waist, actually giving me one. I stroked the soft material. I loved the colour of it, hung it on a hanger on the back of my bedroom door where I could look at it. It made me think of summer skies.

The Monday before the half-term week-end arrived. I wrapped myself up warmly, made sure I didn't get my feet wet. Imagine the anguish if I got a cold and was not allowed to go at the last minute! In the month of February there was no lack of colds and influenza doing the rounds.

Harriet came into school with her face shining.

"They're going to let me go," she cried. "Isn't that great?"

We were astonished for a moment but quickly accepted this about-turn on the Lintons' part, not questioning it. I remember thinking that it was a bit odd but then forgot it. Now, looking back, I think the Lintons let her go because it suited them. They had an engagement at Portstewart for the week-end that did not include Harriet. It was a decision they were to regret.

The days moved slowly by, but at last it was Thursday evening and I was packing. My mother folded the blue dress carefully, interleaving it with tissue paper. The day was cold and the rain coming down thick and straight like stair rods. We didn't care!

Mr MacCabe drove us to the station. I was a bit surprised by Mrs MacCabe's get-up until Sally explained. She was wearing a moth-eaten looking coat, an old felt hat that drooped round the brim, and a pair of shoes that were cracked and split and down at the heel. She looked as if she'd got dressed up in the left-overs from a jumble sale for a laugh. Normally she dressed smartly, was what my mother called 'clothes conscious'. And her sister was dressed similarly. Sally whispered to me that they didn't intend to come home in those clothes, they'd throw them away at the hotel, and come back in brand-new outfits which they meant to purchase in Dublin. They had their suitcases full of tea for that purpose.

You could smell the tea. Its pungent odour filled the car. I sat in the back squashed between Sally and her Auntie Nell wondering if they were going to barter with it, the way they used to do in the Middle Ages. Trade you two pounds of tea for a pair of shoes? It didn't sound too likely to me. But then I hadn't been to Dublin before, didn't know the ropes. Harriet didn't seem put out by it, she was sitting at the window gazing out at the cars swishing through the rain with her usual composure.

"Have a good time then," said Mr MacCabe, as he handed us out of the car. "And see you don't break the Bank of Ireland while you're at it." He chuckled. "Or get arrested by the Customs."

The station was busy for a wet Friday in February. Of course it was half-term at most of the schools. There was a queue for the Dublin train and standing at the head of it beside the barrier was Fraulein Berg.

We didn't get into the same carriage as Fraulein Berg. By the time we struggled up the platform with our luggage we saw that she was sitting in a seat by the window and already a man and woman were settling themselves opposite her. We more or less needed a compartment to ourselves — it was a corridor train with compartments that seated six, or at a pinch, eight — and we got it. I daresay no one who glanced in would have been anxious to join us. We were making enough noise for fifty people, let alone five, and it took us a while to get ourselves sorted out. The suitcases had to be hoisted up on to the rack, our outer clothing removed, including Mrs MacCabe's shoes for the cracks across the front of them were digging into her feet something dreadful, and the picnic had to be laid out. Although the journey could be accomplished between meals, we had to have food and drink with us, or at least any decent member of the MacCabe clan would.

"You never know though, do you?" said Mrs MacCabe. "I mean to say, we could get held up at the Customs for hours."

"Not going this way surely?" said Auntie Nell. "It's

only coming back they're bothered about."

We were certainly not thinking about coming back.

There was no table so we arranged the food on the seat between Sally's mother and aunt. It looked tempting: sausage rolls, sandwiches, butterfly cakes, flies cemeteries. We weren't to start before the train left the station, said Mrs MacCabe, wriggling her toes and sighing with relief. I noticed she was wearing ancient lisle stockings too, with holes in the toes.

The train filled up. Sally and Harriet and I hung out of the window in turns to watch the people going up and down the platform. The station smelt of soot and smoke. And then the guard blew his whistle and raised his green flag.

"Pull your head in for dear sake, Kate," said Auntie Nell. "You don't want to get it taken off, do you?"

"Not before she gets to Dublin at any rate," said Sally.

We fell on the sausage rolls and sandwiches demolishing most of them. The sweet stuff could be left for later, we decided, once we'd crossed the border. The border! What a thrill the words gave me!

Then we went to the toilet. We must have gone to the toilet about a dozen times on the journey and each time we did, we went past Fraulein Berg's compartment so that we could check up on her. On every occasion but one there she was sitting in her corner seat, head down, reading a book.

"Where do you think she's skipped off to? said Sally when we didn't see her.

"The toilet," suggested Harriet.

That was where she was. As we reached it we saw that the door daid 'Engaged'. At that moment the sign shifted backwards to become 'Vacant' and our German teacher emerged.

"Good afternoon, Fraulein Berg," we chanted.

"Good afternoon, girls," she replied curtly.

I don't suppose our presence gave her a very good send-off

for her half-term week-end.

"Have you girls got a chill or something?" asked Mrs MacCabe when we returned.

"'Deed I hope not," said Auntie Nell. "It would be queer inconvenient at the hotel if you did."

We reassured them. They dozed off to sleep. I didn't know how they could. We were much too excited to sit still so when we weren't going to the toilet we were going in and out of the corridor and leaning against the window there, flattening our noses on it and watching the long plume of smoke the train was leaving behind. It was gradually growing dark, the landscape was turning a filmy grey, and I was not going to see very much of Eire, not on this trip. And by the time we reached Dublin it would be dark.

We speculated on why the Fraulein would be going to Dublin. To report to headquarters, no doubt. I remembered the letter with the Eire postmark on her sideboard.

There was no trouble or delay going over the border, as Auntie Nell had predicted. They had pretty well everything they needed down there so smuggling was a one-way business. The only thing they were short of was tea, Harriet explained to me, and the Customs wouldn't be bothered lifting people for running that in. They did have some rationing in the south but it wasn't very strict. My mother had asked me to get one or two things for her, like zips which were in short supply, and some nylon stockings.

The border behind us, we ate the butterfly cakes and flies cemeteries. After that we played noughts and crosses and consequences for a while as Sally's mother and aunt were beginning to complain about the number of times we were opening and shutting the door and letting the draughts in. The last twenty minutes of the journey seemed interminable. And then the lights of Dublin began to appear. The lights! It was quite amazing to see streets threaded with glistening yellow lights and uncurtained windows shining like beacons.

We jumped up and hauled down the luggage standing on one another's feet and getting in one another's way. Mrs MacCabe found that her feet had swollen and she could hardly get them squashed into the shoes.

"Glory be!" she gasped. "I can hardly arrive at the hotel in my stocking feet, can I now?"

Sally pushed and shoved and eventually got them on for her, although there was quite a bit of foot left hanging over the edges.

"I'll never manage to walk." She tried a few steps between the seats whilst we held our own legs up in the air, and collapsed. We all doubled up with laughter, herself included.

"You look like one of them Chinese with the bound feet," said Auntie Nell.

The train was slowing, we must hurry up. We didn't want to be last off.

"We certainly don't," said Mrs MacCabe. "We've got business to transact."

The train steamed into Amiens Street station and shuddered to a halt. We had the window open and Auntie Nell's hand was on the outside handle ready to push it down. We tumbled out.

"Quick, girls!" urged Auntie Nell, unnecessarily.

She took her sister's elbow and helped her along; we carried most of the luggage amongst the three of us. We didn't have time now to look for Fraulein Berg.

As soon as we were through the barrier the 'shawlies' were upon us. The 'shawlies' were women in black shawls and they took me completely by surprise. I had never seen such poor people in such numbers — in Belfast you might have seen the odd one or two about — but these were in flocks, like black birds with talons extended. In their talons they held books of clothing coupons. I hadn't realised that it was with them that our business would be transacted.

Mrs MacCabe, who now seemed to have re-gained control

of her feet, led the way over to the side of the station. A troop of women and small children followed us. The smell coming from them was another thing I had never experienced before. Harriet was holding her nose.

"It's the Roman Catholic church," she whispered. "It makes them all have about twenty children."

"It's no wonder they're poor," said I, looking round.

"Don't look round!" She tugged my sleeve. "You'll just encourage them."

It seemed to me that they had had plenty of encouragement from Mrs MacCabe who had indicated that they were to follow. We stopped at a bench out of the way of the crowds and she and her sister laid their suitcases down flat and flipped up the locks.

"Stand back, girls," said Auntie Nell.

Harriet wandered a few yards off but I stayed as close as I could, not wanting to miss anything. The 'shawlies' were elbowing one another out of the way trying to get nearer to the centre of the action and the small children clinging to their skirts jiggled along behind them. The bargaining began. Mrs MacCabe was brilliant at it. She'd hold up two half-pounds of tea and a woman would make an offer and she'd shake her head and the woman would make another offer, a better one. I could only understand what Mrs MacCabe said, the women spoke in such thick Dublin accents that I could hardly make out more than a few words here and there. What I did gather was that they were starving and their children were starving and they desperately needed money.

"Don't believe everything they say," said Harriet, returning to join us for a brief interval. "My father says they'd lie the heads off themselves for money."

"But they *look* as if they need it."

Harriet veered away again, wrinkling her nose as she went.

Tea and clothing coupons changed hands. Mrs MacCabe and Auntie Nell were kept busy for the next quarter of an hour until the last quarter pound of tea found its way under a black shawl. They snapped the locks of the empty suitcases shut, stowed the books of coupons in their handbags.

"What lovely childer," said one very old woman, turning to smile at me. She had only two teeth left in her mouth and her skin was wrinkled and etched with black lines of dirt. She stretched forward a thin scrawny hand and touched my coat, wanting to stroke it. I backed away.

"That's it!" announced Mrs MacCabe in a loud voice. "Finished." She waved her hand to make it clear that they should go now. Most did, though one or two remained to beg for money.

"Sure you could spare us a shillin', missus. My man's ill and out of work."

"In the jail more than likely," said Auntie Nell.

I slipped a shilling out of my purse and put it into the outstretched hand of the old 'shawlie' who had tried to stroke my coat.

"You shouldn't have done that," said Harriet.

"I'll do what I want, " I retorted.

"Harriet's right," said Auntie Nell quietly. "We'll never get them off our backs."

We traversed the station like pied pipers with a following of 'shawlies' and their offspring trailing along in our wake. One or two of the older children ran ahead pleading for tanners. Mrs MacCabe and Auntie Nell walked smartly with their heads up pretending they didn't hear a word. We were saved by a member of the civil guard, the Irish police force. As soon as he waved the women off they dispersed like autumn leaves blown by the wind. Apparently they weren't allowed to come into the station and bother the passengers coming off the Belfast train. Trading in clothing coupons was not encouraged though they must have known it went on every time a train came in from the North. I imagine they gave them a certain length of time to make their transactions and then came in to clear the station.

The policeman bowed to us.

"Thank you, Officer," said Mrs MacCabe. She rewarded him with a full, beaming smile.

We joined the queue at the taxi rank.

"What'll they do with all that tea?" I asked Sally, not wishing to ask Harriet anything. "They can't drink it surely?"

Sally laughed. "They'll sell it, stupid. At Black Market prices."

I had a vision of a huge covered market, all black, outside and in, and faceless people moving to and fro in the darkness offering pounds of tea and sides of meat to one another, although I did know of course that that was not how it worked at all. It was more the way Mr MacCabe did things: somebody knocked on the door and asked if you were needing anything. My vision was more romantic, I thought, or at least it was as long as it remained dark inside the market. If you were to switch the lights on and see all the 'shawlies' in their darned shawls and the children in their ragged clothes any notion of romance would fly out of the window.

A taxi came and took us out into the streets of Dublin. The lights astonished me anew. I thought the city glittered like something out of fairyland.

The hotel was everything I expected it to be: comfortable, smoothly run, odourless, and the tablecloths were crisp and white and totally lacking in stains of any kind. Not that we saw the dining room until the next morning at breakfast-time for we were not eating dinner there. We were booked in for bed and breakfast. For our evening meal we went to a café in O'Connell Street which was only five minutes walk away. We had bacon, sausage and egg, and then went to Cafola's for Knickerbocker Glories. After that we had to walk it off which we were perfectly happy to do.

We were not the only ones on O'Connell Street. It was ideal for promenading up and down as it was long and wide and there were shop windows to look in and hotels to pass where people were going in and out dressed in fur coats and laughing and obviously having a good time.

"This is what it'll be like in Belfast once the war's over," said Mrs MacCabe. "When the lights go on again."

We had to stop every few yards so that she and her sister could gawk at the shop windows. They kept seeing lovely wee suits and gorgeous dresses and shoes of every colour of the rainbow such as you never saw at home. I was not so interested in the clothes, just wanted to look about me and wonder at the lights and enjoy the strangeness of the place. Sally and Harriet and I *were* interested in the sweet shop windows; we stood and drooled and picked out the boxes of chocolates we would like to buy.

"Come on, you three!" cried Mrs MacCabe.

We drifted along letting ourselves go with the ebb and flow of the crowd for a while then breaking away to go to the wall, to another set of lighted windows. I couldn't help thinking that Hollywood could not be *much* better than this. I said so to Sally and Harriet.

"There's no film stars around but," said Sally.

I was not so sure. Some of the people we passed looked as if they might be. Whenever I gave Belfast a fleeting thought it appeared to me as a dull grey blur.

"When I grow up I'm going to come and live here," I said.

"You must be off your head," said Sally. I questioned that. "Why, it's run by the Papists," she went on. "You wouldn't want to live in a place where you were swamped by them, would you?"

I shrugged.

"Sure it's all right for a visit. But not to *live*."

"I think Hollywood would be safer," said Harriet.

They were off on a favourite topic. I let them get on with it — I didn't feel like thinking about Hollywood tonight, not with this magical city at my feet. I gazed up at the dark statue of Nelson on his pillar (since removed), I watched the tramcars running up the middle of the street, I listened to the Southern Irish voices all around us. Some spoke in Gaelic, not a word of which could I decipher. We didn't hear a single voice speaking in German, not that day.

Eventually the grown-ups tired. We three never would have done, would have walked all night had we been allowed. But we were not.

"We don't want to be too late in our beds," said Sally's

mother. "After all, we've a big day on tomorrow."

We turned up Grafton Street and went into our hotel. The doorman smiled at us and said, "Good evening, ladies." When we had arrived he had carried up our luggage, or some of it. Mrs MacCabe and Auntie Nell had two suitcases each with them, one which had contained the tea and was by then empty although still smelling strongly of it, and another one which I presumed contained some kind of clothing. They had surrendered those cases to him, saying they would just hold on to the others themselves since they weren't heavy. He had insisted on taking Harriet's case under his arm as well as a hold-all. I was amazed at how much he could handle. Mrs MacCabe had given him a tip after he'd showed us into our rooms. She had a separate purseful of coins which she kept for tipping.

Sally and Harriet and I were sharing a room, and a bed. It was a double one so Mrs MacCabe said we should be able to manage since none of us was all that fat. She laughed and slapped her own hip which was none too slender. She told us not to stay awake all night talking and then she and her sister retreated to their room which was further down the passage. Just as well, said Sally, locking the door: they wouldn't be able to hear us. For we had every intention of talking all night.

We were to spend three nights at the hotel so each of us would have a turn in the middle of the bed. Sally was going to take the first night. First we washed at the wash basin in the room and dried ourselves on the clean white towels. In the guest house at Portrush we'd got our water in a china jug and basin. By the time the maid carried it up to us the water had gone cold and both my mother and I had to use the same water. I took my time washing, did my neck thoroughly, and behind my ears. Quite a different performance from my usual lick and promise.

"Hurry up, Kate," called Sally from the bed. "You're

110

not Esther Williams, you know."

The bed was beautifully comfortable and the sheets were clean and smelled of lavender.

"Well, of course they're clean, idiot," said Harriet. "What else would you expect? They wouldn't dare give us dirty linen now, would they?"

I was not sure what they would dare to do, such was my inexperience.

We talked of everything we could think of, Dublin, the shops, the beggars, friends at school, Hollywood — yes, that too, again! — and of course Fraulein Berg. We imagined her abroad in the streets tonight keeping secret assignations, passing documents, moving freely and unchallenged. She was now in neutral territory after all, a concept I found difficult to grasp. Here, Germany was no longer the Enemy. For the last four years it had been the most hated country in the world for us, except possibly Japan, but since that was far away it didn't have the same significance. And Japanese spies in Britain were unheard of, at least by us, though we didn't know what went on in London. A lot of news was censored, said Harriet; her father kept hearing things that never got into the newspapers or on the wireless. She told us a story about a nun being a German spy (or a German spy being dressed up as a nun) and carrying secret documents underneath all that black drapery they got themselves up in. They had been known to do a bit of smuggling too, carrying jewellery and goodness knows what else on their bodies. They had thought they were safe, you see, said Harriet, that no one would suspect them or dare search them.

"But they did?" I asked.

Harriet nodded. "And the things they found! You wouldn't believe it."

"Were they searched by men?" I asked.

"Oh no, they couldn't get away with that. They have

lady searchers on the border too."

"It must be awful to get searched."

"Imagine having all your clothes taken off and being made to stand there stark naked!"

The idea made us giggle. Sally thought that everybody was lined up in the same room and stripped and searched but Harriet was dubious.

"It could be a real gas, couldn't it?" said Sally. "To be taken off the train for searching?"

"Do you think so?" said Harriet.

Was it likely, I wanted to know, that one would be taken off the train? Not at all, said Harriet; they had to suspect you first. Her father said they were usually acting on tip-offs. Some Dublin jewellers, if they had made a big sale to someone from the North, might pass on the news to the Customs. And then they would be on the look out for him.

"A friend of Mum's was searched once," said Sally. "She was wearing a new fur coat and they lifted it off her."

"She couldn't have been very smart," said Harriet.

I yawned and the infection spread to the other two. Gradually our voices got softer and slower. Somebody in the next room was running water. Footsteps passed our door. A car swished by in the street and was gone. The city was quietening, dimming down for the night, and only the civil guard, tramps, late revellers, and German spies were left to walk its streets.

I wakened to see sunlight coming through a chink in the curtains to make a streak of gold on the floor. The other two slept half lying on top of one another. I crept out of bed, careful not to disturb them, and went to the window. I eased the curtain back a fraction and peered out. It was a glorious crisp winter day. Above the rooftops I saw blue sky smudged with traces of pink and pale green. People were walking on the pavement below, going to work, or perhaps they were just out enjoying the beautiful morning in a beautiful city.

112

"Wake up!" I cried. "The sun's shining."

The grown-ups were already up and waiting to go down for breakfast. We dressed hastily, not bothering so much about the washing this time. For breakfast we had bacon, sausages and egg. The sausages were from Hafners, said Mrs MacCabe, and they were the best sausages in the whole wide world, not excepting her own husband's. I had to agree with her. They were so delicious they just melted in your mouth. Of course they could put more real meat in them here, said Auntie Nell; they didn't have to stuff them out with all that rubbish that we did at home.

Mrs MacCabe dispensed tea from the silver teapot and refilled it with water from a silver jug. We sat up very straight and asked one another to pass this and that. Somehow grabbing would not have entered your mind in a place like that. At the MacCabes' house nobody had time for passing: it was a case of diving in and may the fastest survive. Mrs MacCabe and Auntie Nell also sat with their backs held straighter than usual. The only thing that wasn't right about them was their clothing. They each wore a jumper and skirt which my mother would have described as having seen better days. But it was the last time I was to see them thus attired.

They were full of shopping plans.

"We're going to make a real day of it," said Mrs MacCabe. "And tomorrow we'll take you to the zoo or Dun Laoghaire." Being Sunday the shops would not be open anyway. She said she would let us amuse ourselves for the day as long as we promised not to stray too far from the centre.

"They'll be all right, Millie," said Auntie Nell. "They're getting to be big girls now, after all."

We were delighted to be released from the shopping tour and promised to be sensible and cautious, not to speak to strangers or wander up lonely alleyways. An arrangement was made for us to meet up for lunch. Underneath Nelson's pillar at one o'clock.

"You can't miss that," said Sally's mother.

She called for another pot of tea and two more rounds of toast. They needed to stock up, build their strength for the ordeal ahead. The shopping expedition sounded a bit like an endurance test.

We walked down to O'Connell Street with them and then split up. We watched them walk off and disappear into the crowd.

For a moment or two we didn't know what to do with ourselves. Passers-by milled around jostling us with their shopping bags. It looked as though the entire population of Dublin was out buying new outfits that morning.

"Let's go and get some sweets," said Sally.

Her suggestion unfroze us and we went briskly in the direction of a confectioner whose window we had surveyed the night before with covetous eyes. It took us quite a while to make a choice. I could still hardly believe that we didn't have to produce sweet coupons, that we could say we would have this and this and this, as long as we had money to spend. We bought some several small things and one large box of chocolates to share amongst us.

"We could go to St. Stephen's Green to eat them," said Harriet. "I think I can remember the way."

She did. We sat down on a bench and Sally tore the cellophane wrapping off the box. She lifted the lid, removed the paper which told you what the centres were. We pored over it reading the names aloud. Vanilla fudge. Raspberry cream. Russian caramel.

I glanced sideways aware of something black coming between me and the sun. A priest had come to sit on the end of our bench. Sally dug me in the ribs and I looked back at her and the chocolates. She made a face letting me know what she thought about having to share a park bench with a priest of the Church of Rome.

"Let's have one then," said Harriet impatiently.

114

We chose in turn, each taking a few minutes to make the big decision. I started with a caramel which stuck to my teeth and made me chew vigorously. I liked the hard centres best, Sally favoured the creams, and Harriet had a wide taste, so we didn't quarrel. It was only when we got down to the bottom of the box that the choosing began to be a problem. None of us cared for nut cracknel or Turkish delight. The birds might, I suggested. There were dozens of little starlings hovering around us, their beady eyes flicking over the box. But Harriet and Sally thought that chocolates were too special to give away to birds.

"Are you enjoying yourselves then, girls?" said a voice beside me.

I almost dropped my vanilla fudge. It was the priest who was addressing us. I had to look round. He had a red smiling face and twinkly black eyes.

"Yes, thank you," I said primly.

Afterwards, Harriet and Sally said I shouldn't have answered as it just encouraged him.

"Fond of chocolates, are you?"

"Yes."

"You're not from Dublin, eh?"

"No."

Sally dug me hard in the ribs and I winced, slightly winded.

"From the North, are you?"

"Yes."

I had been brought up to speak when spoken to. I did not know how to ignore a direct question.

"What's it like up there these days?"

"All right," I said lamely.

At this point Harriet got up. "It's time we were going to meet your mother, Sally," she said in a loud voice.

"Cheerio," said the priest.

"Cheerio," said I.

I followed Sally and Harriet into St. Stephen's Street.

"What did you have to get into conversation with a priest for?" demanded Sally, as soon as we were out of his hearing.

"He seemed harmless enough."

"Harmless!" Sally snorted. "He was probably out to convert us."

"Don't be daft. How would he even know we were Protestants to start with?"

"Oh, they know all right. They can tell. You can tell a Catholic, can't you?"

That was true and I had to admit it. It's an odd thing that people who haven't been brought up in the North of Ireland might not understand. What it was exactly that enabled one to make the distinction I don't quite know. Perhaps it was simply that we had grown up looking for the differences. Once I gave the point away to Sally she had won the argument. I let it go. She said it was just as well her mother hadn't seen me, she'd have had a blue fit. I knew Mr MacCabe would have blown his top but I could not imagine his wife having a blue fit over a thing like that; she had remained calm through a lot worse happenings, even when a German bomb fell twenty yards from their house and lay, unexploded, in a crater in the roadway. She had taken her time about evacuating herself and made sure she got the best stuff out of her wardrobe first. No German bomb was going to demolish her musquash coat and black moiré taffeta evening gown.

We forgot the priest in St. Stephen's Green although we saw many others in the streets, as well as nuns. Whenever we passed any Sally looked away.

"Where are we going now?" I asked.

"What about the German Embassy?" said Harriet.

That was an idea that appealed to us. Goodness knows what we might see going on there! With a bit of luck we would catch a glimpse of Fraulein Berg.

"She might be having morning coffee with the Ambassador," said Harriet.

116

We had to ask the way which we felt a bit awkward about. People might think we were Germans.

"You ask, Harriet," said Sally. "You're good at asking."

Harriet stopped a little old lady who we thought looked safe.

"The German what?" she said, cupping her ear.

"Embassy," shouted Harriet, growing red in the face.

"'Deed I never heard of the place."

The woman shuffled on. A civil guard came past, strolling unhurriedly, swinging his stick. We certainly could not ask him for he might ask us what we wanted to know for.

We solved the problem by asking at a newsagent's. The woman looked at us a bit oddly but called over to the man, "Do you know where the German Embassy is, Dermot?" Dermot came to the door and pointed the way.

"Got business there, eh?" he said with a grin.

Harriet tilted her head up. "Thank you very much," she said.

We followed his instructions, found it easily. There it was, with its eagle over the door and the German flag flying! We caught our breath.

"What a nerve!" said Sally.

We stood across the street and stared at it. Inside that building a group of Germans was probably planning and plotting the downfall of the United Kingdom.

"They might well be looking at a plan for invading the North right now," said Harriet.

We could imagine them, seated round a table on which was spread the map of Ireland. They would be wearing swastika armbands and every time the door opened they would jump to their feet shouting, 'Heil Hitler!' and give that hated salute.

A man came down the steps and walked off along the street. He was wearing an ordinary suit and no hat. They would take their armbands off before coming out, said

117

Harriet; they wouldn't want to attract too much attention. Of Fraulein Berg there was no sign, either in the street or at any of the windows. We stood until our feet numbed and we had to stamp them to keep the circulation going.

Two men were coming out of the Embassy now. And they were crossing the road coming towards us!

"Glory be!" said Sally softly. "Maybe they're after us. *She* might have sent them."

The men stopped in front of us.

"Do you wish anything?" asked one.

"No," I faltered.

"We have noticed you have been looking."

It was not a question so I didn't answer.

The men spoke to one another in German and then they turned, with a curt nod to us, and went down the street. We scuttled off, fast, in the opposite direction.

"That was a near escape," said Harriet. "They might have tried to kidnap us. They could have hidden us inside the Embassy and your mother would never have guessed where we were."

Now that we were safe we were able to enjoy the encounter, in retrospect. By the time we had finished talking about it we were convinced they *had* tried to kidnap us and we had foiled them in their attempt.

"We'll need to keep our eyes peeled," said Sally. "You never know — they might be looking for us now."

Mrs MacCabe and Auntie Nell were waiting under Nelson's pillar with a cluster of shopping bags.

"We've been buying the place up," said Auntie Nell. "Wait till you see all we've bought!"

We went to Bewleys Oriental Café for our lunch. A snack would do us rightly, said Mrs MacCabe, and then we could have a big meal in the evening. We went through the outer shop into the restaurant. It was huge and unlike any café I had been in before. The wallpaper was oriental and there were Chinese vases everywhere. We sat down at a rectangular table with a glass top. The place was packed. Everybody came to Bewleys, said Mrs MacCabe, kicking off her shoes under the table. They were new. The cracked ones had found a resting place in some Dublin litter bin.

Everybody included Fraulein Berg. She was sitting in a corner with another woman. She looked up from her coffee cup and saw us.

I would just as soon not have seen Fraulein Berg drinking coffee in Bewleys Oriental Café. I would have liked a rest from her as, no doubt, she would have liked one from us. She must have felt we were haunting her.

Fortunately, she left only a few minutes later. She got up and walked out without glancing in our direction, her friend at her heels. Her friend looked much as she did, dark, with nothing out of the way about her. Immediately Harriet and Sally put their heads together and began to whisper. I sat back in my chair and surveyed the room. There was nothing I liked better than to watch people coming and going.

After lunch the ladies resumed their onslaught on the shops and the three of us did what shopping we intended to do. I bought a dozen zips of varying sizes and colours and two pairs of nylon stockings for my mother, and a box of chocolates and a book for myself.

"You can get books in Belfast," said Sally.

But I wanted to bring a book back from Dublin as a memento of the week-end. I knew the chocolates wouldn't survive very long. Mrs MacCabe said she was going to buy Sally some shoes so we had to go with her first but once they were purchased we were released to pursue our own activities again. We gave the German Embassy a wide birth, went to Phoenix Park, and rode up and down the city in tramcars.

As the afternoon light was beginning to dwindle we returned to the hotel. Mrs MacCabe and Auntie Nell were back in their rooms having a fashion parade. They had bought new suits, coats, skirts, jumpers, shoes, apart from a whole heap of underwear. Sally and Harriet and I sat on the bed and they paraded up and down the middle of the room, their hands on their hips, saying things like, "This is the latest creation from Paris. Notice the back pleat. . ." We had great fun. I laughed until I thought I might be sick, which was not an impossibility since we had eaten more or less non-stop all day. Sweets, chocolates, cakes, sausages, whipped cream. I thought I would never eat another bite but when we went out for our evening meal I managed to. And after it we went to the cinema.

"We need to give our feet a rest," said Mrs MacCabe.

She and Auntie Nell fell asleep half way through the main feature. Their snores could be heard in the quiet bits. What a waste! I couldn't understand how anyone could sleep through Ginger Rogers and Fred Astaire.

We fell asleep as soon as our heads hit the pillow that night; we said no more than a few words to one another once the light was out.

Sunday was another day of bright blue skies and golden sunshine. Frost still lay on the grass as we walked in the early morning on St. Stephen's Green. Of our priest there was no sign. He would be in his church saying mass.

Mrs MacCabe said a Dublin Sunday was not half as dead as a Belfast one, thank goodness for that. At least not after twelve noon. Why was that? I asked. "Oh, they only keep Sunday up till midday. They go to mass in the morning, you see, and then they can do anything they like afterwards. They don't have to live like saints all day."

We saw plenty of people heading for the churches. Bells rang out across the city. In Belfast the church bells had not been heard since the war started: they were being kept silent in case of invasion. If the bells were to ring you'd know the Enemy was coming.

"Sunday's the same on the Continent of course," said Auntie Nell, who had never set foot on foreign soil, except for that of Eire, and I was not sure whether she would count that as foreign or not. "They go to mass and then they can do what they like afterwards with a clear conscience." She shook her head in a way that suggested the living up involved a good deal of wickedness.

"They can't do what they want now though, can they?" said I. "I mean, with the Germans there. Not in France anyway, or Belgium, or Holland."

"Aye, you're right, Kate. Poor souls! Can't be much fun having the Gerries over you."

I thought that did not express it too well.

"Can you imagine them coming to knock on your door in the middle of the night and taking you away as a hostage?"

"And shooting you at dawn against a wall for harbouring a British airman," added Harriet dramatically. You could tell she'd been having elocution lessons.

Mrs MacCabe shivered. "I don't think we want to be dwelling on things like that today. We're here to enjoy ourselves. And there's nothing we can do for them is there?"

Sally and Harriet and I looked at one another and thought of Fraulein Berg. There might be something we could do, in a small way. To put even one spy out of operation would contribute to the war effort, more than rolling bandages for the Red Cross, or knitting mittens for airmen.

We spent most of the day at Dun Laoghaire, a seaside resort outside Dublin. We walked along the sand and spun stones through the waves. Mrs MacCabe refused to let us paddle.

"Paddle in the month of February? You must be joking! What would your mother say, Harriet, and yours, Kate, if I was to bring you both back suffering from pneumonia?"

In the late afternoon we returned to Dublin. The others were going for coffee and cakes but my stomach was a bit queasy so I said I would just go on back to the hotel if they didn't mind.

"Are you sure you're all right now, Kate?" Mrs MacCabe probably felt she should make a little fuss since I was not her child, but she was not a natural fusser so she let me go.

I was happy to be on my own for one hour. I felt grown-up walking into the hotel on my own answering the doorman's greeting.

"Had a good day, miss?"

"Lovely, thank you."

I decided I would go and sit in the residents' lounge. We had glanced in at it the night we'd arrived when we had cased the hotel. It had looked comfortable and quiet.

I slipped inside. The only occupant, a woman about my mother's age, glanced up at me and smiled. I sank into an armchair and began to read a magazine as she was doing. After a bit we exchanged magazines and she engaged me in conversation. She wanted to know if I was here on holiday, and for long; I gave her a complete run-down on our week-end, though did not mention the big shopping expedition of course. I knew that was top secret. And that the Customs had spies everywhere. Although I could not believe that this woman was a spy, not for a second. She was terribly nice. She had five children of her own and she told me all about them and showed me photographs. They lived in Cork. She was here for a week-end with her husband. They were going to the theatre, doing some shopping and visiting friends.

"A week-end in Dublin is always very enjoyable."

I agreed fervently.

"You must visit Cork sometime."

I said that I would when I was grown up and could afford it. I intended to travel all over Ireland, to see the Mountains of Wicklow, the Vale of Tralee, the Rings of Kerry, and kiss the Blarney stone! We laughed.

We got on to the war then. She said she hoped it wouldn't be too long till it was all over for us.

I was not sure how to take that remark. Did she mean she hoped it would not be long until the Germans had defeated us? According to Sally, everybody in the South wanted the Germans to win, although my mother often said that everybody was a big word and one should be careful how one used it.

For a moment I hesitated and then decided to be bold. "Who do you want to win?" I asked.

She looked a little astonished. "Why, the British of course."

"But I thought — well, that you were all on the Germans' side?"

"A few are, no doubt. But most reasonable Irishmen and women would not be wanting a man like Hitler to conquer Europe. Once he was in the North of Ireland he'd be down here after that. Do you think we'd like that?"

I shook my head. I was confused. Why did they have the German Embassy here and allow people to chalk swastika slogans on walls? She said they didn't like people writing any kind of slogans on walls and, as for the Embassy, she had to admit that she would have preferred it if they had broken off relations with Germany from the start. I found my conversation with her most interesting and could have stayed for another hour. She told me that the Irish were not too fond of the English because of the Easter Rising. I had heard about it vaguely and once had asked our history teacher and she had told me that it was not on the syllabus. We didn't study Irish history. Most of our teachers could not see beyond their syllabuses. The woman told me that in 1916, at Easter, there had been a rising at the Post Office of people wanting independence. This had been brutally put down by the English.

"It's left a few scars." She sighed. "It'll take a while for them to heal. Just as your war with Germany will."

Those scars would never heal, I was convinced of that. How could people who had fought so bitterly ever become friends? At that point her husband arrived and she had to go.

"If you ever come to Cork come and visit us. Have you a card on you, Cormack?"

He gave me his card and we said goodbye. It was the first time anyone had ever given me their card. I read the name on it. Cormack O'Hagan. A truly Irish name if ever there was one, and a Catholic one at that. It was funny but in that hour I'd been with her it had never crossed my mind to wonder if she was Protestant or Catholic, and, if it had, I knew I would not have been able to decide. I put the card in my pocket and said nothing about her to Harriet or Sally.

We had a busy evening ahead.

We gathered in the grown-ups' room and Mrs MacCabe locked the door. Auntie Nell was laying out on the bed all the stuff they had bought. The curtains were drawn tightly across the window with as much care as we gave to our blackouts at home. You couldn't be too careful, said Mrs MacCabe, and we should not talk about what we were doing even though the door was locked. People had been known to listen at keyholes before now.

She took from her suitcase a pair of scissors, a packet of sewing needles, two reels of thread, one light, one dark, and a bundle of old labels from shops in Belfast. Robinson and Cleavers. Anderson and McCauley. The Bank Buildings. There was also a number of the little utility labels which were white with a black design on them. I didn't ask what she intended to do with them, I was soon going to find out.

125

She took the jacket of her new suit and carefully snipped the label from the inside of the collar. Then she picked up one that said 'Robinson and Cleaver' and began to sew that in its place.

"You'd never be a bit the wiser now, would you?" she said, holding it up for us to admire.

I was full of admiration for her cleverness though I was not sure my mother would approve.

We were allowed to do some sewing too though were cautioned that we must use the teeniest of stitches so that they would look professionally done. The thing was not to attract attention, said Auntie Nell, who was working busily herself. Mrs MacCabe also instructed me to sew my mother's zips inside the lining of my coat.

"It'll be queer and uncomfortable for her sitting on that lot," giggled Sally.

You had to be prepared to put up with a bit of discomfort sometimes, her mother told her. "Anyway, you're going to have to put your shoes down the arms of your coat. I'm not wanting to throw away the ones you've got on — there's plenty of life in them yet."

It took us until bedtime to get everything ready for the Customs. But Mrs MacCabe was well pleased with our efforts.

"They'd need to be pretty smart to catch us with this lot," she said.

We had most of Monday left and now could relax since all the chores were done. We were leaving on an early evening train so that we would squeeze as much time as we could out of our week-end. Before leaving for the station we had a last guzzle of cream cakes and peach melbas.

Fraulein Berg was waiting at the barrier for the Belfast train. We might have expected her to be on this one, wanting to have as long a holiday as possible also.

"Look, there's her friend!" said Harriet. "The one she was in Bewleys with."

We spun around to see the woman hurrying across the station towards the queue.

"Maybe she's going with her," I said.

But she was not. She had come to give Fraulein Berg a package! It was slim and about six inches long, as far as we could make out by craning our necks.

"What are you looking at, girls?" asked Mrs MacCabe.

"Nothing," we chorused.

Fraulein Berg seemed embarrassed. Her face was pink and she was talking with animation. Then the man came to open the barrier and let us on to the platform. Quickly, she flipped open her suitcase and slid the package in. She and her friend embraced, the man who was second in the queue pushed past them, and we all moved forward. We found ourselves going up the platform abreast of our German teacher.

She stepped up into a carriage; Mrs MacCabe followed, saying we didn't want to walk too far up the train. Fraulein Berg went into an empty compartment, put her suitcase up on the rack beside the window.

"This'll do as well as any other," said Mrs MacCabe.

We bundled in behind her with our cases and bags. Fraulein Berg did not look at all happy to see that we were to be her travelling companions.

"Hello," we said limply.

Mrs MacCabe beamed at her. "You know the girls then, do you?"

Fraulein Berg admitted to teaching us German.

"You don't say? It's a small world, isn't it? And how's Sally doing at the German?"

"Quite well," said Fraulein Berg, which was a lie. Sally couldn't get the hang of it at all. The subject of the discussion had to face about to avoid the teacher's eyes. We didn't take off our coats because we couldn't. It was going to be a warm journey.

Fraulein Berg opened her book and thus discouraged any

further conversation. Mrs MacCabe looked a little put out but shrugged her shoulders.

Auntie Nell sat beside the Fraulein but I had to sit opposite which was much worse. I hesitated to lift my eyes above her knees. We were quiet as we sat and waited for the train to pull out, in contrast to our noisy departure from Belfast.

"I reckon you'll sleep well the night, girls," said Mrs MacCabe, stretching out her legs decked in their new nylon stocking.

When we were five minutes out of Dublin, Fraulein Berg closed her book and rose. She pulled down her suitcase. I thought she must have decided to take herself off and find another compartment but she merely opened the lid and removed the packet her friend had given her. Sally and Harriet and I eyed one another. She re-closed the suitcase, placed it back on the rack, and put the parcel in her handbag. Then she said, "Excuse me," and edged between our legs towards the door.

"I think I'll go to the toilet," said Sally.

"Already?" said her mother.

Harriet and I said we would go with her. We scuttled along the corridor to find the engaged sign on the toilet door. We moved back a couple of feet.

"She must be in there," whispered Harriet. "She must be doing something with the parcel."

Getting rid of it? I suggested, but Harriet could not see much sense in that. She was convinced the package contained some kind of secret that was to be passed to someone in Belfast. "You must admit there's something fishy about it."

"She seemed bothered about it right enough," I agreed. And even when she had taken it from her suitcase I had noticed a slight blush on her cheeks. Normally her skin was colourless, like parchment paper.

The toilet door opened and out she came. She nodded as

128

she passed us. We stayed out in the corridor so that we could talk freely; also Sally said she found it easier standing up than sitting down with a shoe stuck inside each sleeve of her coat. She couldn't bend her arms.

"Shush!" said Harriet. "Somebody might hear you."

We glanced along the corridor but it was empty save for us. We walked up and down looking through the glass doors into each compartment to see if we could spot spies. Mrs MacCabe had also told us that sometimes people would split on some-one in their compartment to divert attention from themselves. We had heard so many tales about smuggling that my head was reeling and I imagined that nearly everyone on the train was laden with clothes and jewels and pounds of butter. Everyone brought stuff back from Dublin, said Auntie Nell; she'd never heard tell of anyone who didn't. What was the point of going?

I noticed a lot of people were sitting behind books and newspapers that they weren't reading.

"Nerves," said Harriet. "You should see the way everyone sits back and relaxes after they've passed the border."

"That's true," said Sally. "They start talking to one another and passing the chocolates round."

We passed our own compartment again. Mrs MacCabe and her sister were sleeping, their feet up on our vacant seats, displaying their brand new shoes. They should have kept them tucked out of sight. I wondered how smart they really were at this smuggling game. Fraulein Berg's face was hidden behind her book.

"She *is* up to something," said Harriet, not for the first time. We were in the habit of repeating ourselves which did not bore us but would have done anyone else who had to listen. We talked about Fraulein Berg's package and debated what we could do about it.

"We could tip off the Customs man," said Harriet.

"Hey, that's an idea," said Sally.

"Do you think we should?" said I, not because I felt more kindly to Fraulein Berg than they did but probably because I fancied it might be asking for trouble. For ourselves.

"I think we should. It is our duty," said Harriet solemnly. She raised a hand in the Girl Guide salute. "I promise to do my duty to God and the King."

The King would obviously wish us to denounce a German spy. But how were we going to do it? I asked. Did Harriet think we could actually tell the man in front of Fraulein Berg.

"We could write another anonymous letter," said Sally.

I was not going to do it this time. Harriet tossed her head and said that she would, she didn't mind. She tore a page from her diary and we helped steady her whilst she printed the letters: 'In this compartment is a German who is carrying a secret parcel.'

The words looked pretty squiggly from the lurching of the train.

"I'll try to pass it to him as he comes in."

I didn't really think she would do it, not when it came to the crunch. It's like one of those mad ideas that you dream up but never want to see materialise.

"Girls!" Mrs MacCabe's head was poking into the corridor and she was signalling to us. "Come quick! We're near the border."

The train was losing speed. We rushed back to our seats. Sally had to wriggle and jiggle with her sleeves before she could sit down. Fraulein Berg did not seem to be paying any attention.

Nothing much happened at the Eire Customs again. A man in uniform walked up and down glancing in the compartments but he did not open our door at any rate.

"We must look innocent," said Mrs MacCabe, giving Fraulein Berg a smile. The Fraulein gave a very faint one in return.

130

The train chuntered on again not picking up any great speed since it must soon make a second stop. You could almost sense a change in the atmosphere of the whole train when it did come to a halt. I rubbed a patch clear on the window and saw a number of men in dark uniforms standing on the platform.

We had to wait for what seemed like hours. Harriet, who was nearest the door, opened it from time to time, to peep out and give us a report on what was going on. She said she could see a Customs man carrying a whole pile of stuff. And through the window I saw two passengers being led off the train in the direction of the huts.

"They must be doing a thorough search the night," said Auntie Nell. "Ah well, we've nothing to worry about. Fancy a chocolate, girls?"

I didn't fancy anything except to see all those dark suited men disappear into the night and feel the train move off and hear the chuggedy-chug of the wheels beneath us.

"They're just two doors along," announced Harriet.

A minute or so later she got up suddenly saying she'd dropped her handkershief in the corridor. Before Mrs MacCabe could say a word she dived out. I felt the perspiration trickling down my back.

Harriet slid back into her seat. Her face was scarlet and she was trying to look unconcerned. We knew she must have handed over the letter.

"Anything to declare?"

Our turn had come. There were two of them and one was holding something in his hand and frowning. Harriet's note.

"Half a pound of butter," said Mrs MacCabe brightly. She claimed it was better to declare something for they weren't fool enough to think you would have nothing on you.

"Same here," said Auntie Nell, brandishing it. "And the girls have got some chocolates."

"Would you mind letting us see your luggage?"

"Certainly!"

We pulled down our cases and the two men ruffled through them. There was nothing to arouse suspicion in our three cases but the ladies had in theirs some underwear and a skirt and jumper apiece that had been bought in Dublin. One man looked at the labels and pursed his lips. Mrs MacCabe didn't look too worried though I thought I was going to faint for the first time ever. The other man was asking for identity cards. He gave ours a quick glance but when he took Fraulein Berg's into his hand his expression changed. He examined it closely, then looked at her.

"You have nothing to declare, madam?"

"No." She spoke in a very low voice.

He searched her suitcase, found nothing to interest him. He scrawled on it with chalk.

"Wearing any jewellery?"

"A ring." She held out her hand. The ring was a small opal which we had seen before.

"Where did you get it?"

"Berlin. 1935." She lifted her head and spoke more strongly now.

"Have you got a watch?"

That blush returned. I noticed it and wondered if he had. She extended her wrist so that a slim gold watch emerged from under her cuff.

"May I see it?"

She unfastened it. He held it in the palm of his hand.

"Where did you get this?"

"A friend gave it to me," she faltered. "For my birthday."

"A friend in Dublin? You know that presents are not exempt?"

She seemed unable to speak. I wanted to say something but didn't know what to say. What could I say?

And then Sally dropped a shoe out of her sleeve. It fell to the floor with a thump. We all looked down at it, the five

132

of us, Fraulein Berg, and the two Customs men.

"Would you mind removing your coat, miss?"

Sally removed her coat and then they removed us from the train, Fraulein Berg included.

"There's something funny about this whole crowd," said one Customs man to the other. He waved our note in the air. "If you ask me this was meant as a red herring."

Mrs MacCabe protested loudly and indignantly but to no avail. We had to go to the huts and be stripped and searched.

"I've never felt so humiliated in my whole life," Mrs MacCabe declared at intervals throughout the rest of the journey back to Belfast. "You'd think we were *professional* smugglers, when all we had on us were a few bits and pieces."

They were without the bits and pieces now: all had been taken from them except for a skirt and jumper apiece so that they would not have to travel naked. Their legs and feet were bare and were gradually turning purple since the train was not that hot and it was February outside. The air had seemed decidedly cooler since we crossed the border. Maybe they had turned the heating off. We were glad at least of the pulled blinds: we wanted to be shrouded from the world. It was a bit like being in mourning.

Auntie Nell said little but she sighed a lot and shook her head mournfully. Sally, Harriet, and I said nothing. We didn't dare. Nor did we feel like saying anything. And Fraulein Berg was no longer with us. When we had been allowed to return to the train she had taken herself off to another carriage. She had not said a word to any of us even when the Customs man had read out our note. Sally's mother had said plenty. And we, of course, had hung our heads and said we hadn't meant it.

"It was only a joke," muttered Sally.

"A joke?" screamed her mother.

Joke or not, the Customs men were not going to let us slide away without being searched and so we had had to go into a hut and be examined by two women searchers. They found everything, including the zips inside the lining of my coat. They were expert at finding things, knew all the tricks people got up to. They cut Auntie Nell's butter into a dozen peices until they unearthed a ring with a small ruby stone. We hadn't even known she'd had it.

"I just took a notion to it," she said. "I thought I'd treat myself."

The woman laid it, clogged with yellow butter, on the table beside the rest of their haul.

"They'll have a good time the night," said Mrs MacCabe, as we left the hut, "divvying up the spoils." Her sister hushed her, saying we didn't want to get into any more trouble than we were in already.

I thought we were lucky to get away without being locked up. In the middle of the search I had visions of us all behind bars, naked and without food, waiting to be rescued, not by Errol Flynn — somehow he wouldn't fit in to this — but by Harriet's father the lawyer. Harriet's father was a sobering thought and I am sure from the look on Mrs MacCabe's face she was thinking about him herself from time to time.

Fraulein Berg had had nothing illegal on her apart from half a pound of butter and the watch. Both were confiscated.

"You're a hard lot," said Mrs MacCabe to the searchers, who continued, unperturbed, to run their hands inside coat linings and tip out the contents of handbags. Lipsticks and small change rolled in all directions. The three of us went scurrying after them, glad to have something to do other than stand there wishing we were dead. Perhaps not dead, just desperately ill, with a good chance of survival, for then we could lie in bed in shaded rooms and our families would fuss over us full of concern. The fuss they were going to make when we got home was not going to have much concern in it, not for our well-being anyway. It was all our faults, we knew and accepted that, for writing the note and drawing attention to our carriage. Sally's dropping of the shoe had been an accident and for that she could only be called a silly idiot, little more.

We did not go to the toilet at all on the last stretch of the journey. We did not wish to see or be seen by Fraulein Berg, or any of the other passengers. Because of us the train had been held up for a long time and as we walked back along the platform the windows were crammed with faces looking out at us.

"The shame of it," moaned Mrs MacCabe.

The train sped on through the dark countryside of Northern Ireland heading for Belfast. Mr MacCabe was coming to the station to meet us.

"Thank goodness for that at any rate," said his wife. "Just think if we'd to take the bus! And us with our poor freezing feet, Nell."

I would have offered her my shoes and socks except that they would have been far too small.

We were almost there. We could hear activity up and down the train. We didn't move, we were not in any hurry.

"We'll just let them all get off first," said Mrs MacCabe.

So whilst the train came to rest and the passengers disembarked, we continued to sit, arms folded, not daring to look at one another.

Suddenly, our outside door opened and a burst of cold night air rushed in.

"Belfast!" shouted the porter. "You've arrived, ladies. Or are you for spending the night on the train?"

Without a word, her head held high, Mrs MacCabe rose to her feet and lifted down her two empty suitcases.

136

"Are you wanting your luggage carried?"

"No, thank you. We can manage."

Putting one bare foot forward, she stepped down from the train. We followed. Only a few stragglers were left and the platform was shadowy so we did not attract too much attention. And we did not look back to see the porter's face.

Mrs MacCabe gave up the tickets at the barrier and we went through. Her husband was standing there with Mr Linton.

They had been watching for us with that kind of expectant look that people have when they're waiting for someone off a train. As soon as they saw Mrs MacCabe and Auntie Nell their expressions changed. Their eyes went down to their feet and then slowly travelled up their bare legs, over their coatless bodies, to their hatless heads.

"Millie, for dear sake — "

"Now, Dan, don't start! I've had enough for one day. We've just had a bit of bad luck, that's all." She changed her voice before she spoke to Harriet's father. "Oh, good evening, Mr Linton. So nice to see you."

I admired the way she spoke to him as if nothing at all was the matter and it was quite usual for her to arrive at the station in bare feet on a winter's night. But he was no fool and he did not need to have what had happened spelled out to him. He would have heard plenty of tales about people arriving in such a state from Dublin, although it was in-conceivable that it would ever happen to him or his wife.

"Well, Harriet, I think we had better be getting on our way." He was polite, but very very cold, as cold as the night itself. "Your mother will be wondering what's happened to us. Say thank you to Mrs MacCabe."

"Thank you for a lovely week-end," said Harriet.

Once they had left us Mrs MacCabe let fly. She was pretty sure it was that little minx Harriet who had been at the bottom of it; the page had been torn from her diary.

"What page, love?" asked Mr MacCabe.

"We were all to blame," I said miserably, wishing we could just go home. I didn't want to stand in the station any longer and I didn't know how the women could bear the ground on their naked feet. Mrs MacCabe was so worked up about us and the Customs men and the searchers that I daresay her wrath was keeping her warm. I was glad when Auntie Nell said she was dying to get home to her bed.

We passed Fraulein Berg standing outside the station waiting for a bus. It was a bleak night to have to stand on the pavement and although she had not lost her overcoat she could not have been feeling very warm inside. She looked up and saw me sitting at the window on the left hand side of the car. But maybe she didn't. Perhaps it was my feeling of guilt that made me think so.

On the way home Mrs MacCabe told her husband what had happened at the border, excluding any mention of our German teacher. He waxed indignant.

"They've a queer nerve so they have! Leaving you to walk home barefoot. I've a good mind to write to the Customs and Excise so I have."

"I wouldn't do that, Dan," said Auntie Nell from the back seat. "Best let it die a natural death."

"Aye, she's right." Mrs MacCabe sighed, as though she was reluctant to, but would let her better judgment prevail. "You never get anywhere with these officials." She twisted her neck round to look at me. "If I was you, Kate, I wouldn't say too much to your mother. I mean to say, there's no point, is there?"

I could not but agree.

They dropped me off outside my door.

"See you tomorrow, Kate," said Sally.

Tomorrow. School. I could hardly take it in. It seemed a lifetime since we had left home to go to Dublin and I didn't feel like school again so quickly.

"You're late," said my mother, but she was not worried. "Train held up at the border, I suppose?"

I did not have to tell a lie to that question. She made me some cocoa and we sat by the fire so that I could tell her all about it, which I did, at least all about Bewleys and the hotel and St. Stephen's Green.

"Did you get my zips?" she asked, remembering suddenly, and then seeing my face, "Did you forget?"

"No, but — "

"But what?"

"The Customs took them off me."

"Really? I wouldn't have thought they'd have bothered about wee things like that. Ach well! Sometimes they'll let you away with anything and from what I hear another time they'd take the littlest thing off you. It must depend on their mood."

And so I went to bed without having to say anything more about the Customs or having to speak about Fraulein Berg at all. I was so exhausted that I slept at once but the moment I wakened I found she was in my mind. I wondered if she might report us to Miss Thistlethwaite. Sally and I discussed the possibility as we walked down the hill together but we were inclined to feel she would not, that she would want to keep as quiet about the whole business as we did. And we were right. The day passed without us being summoned to the headmistress's room.

"She would have to confess she'd been smuggling too," said Harriet.

"She wasn't really smuggling the watch. Her friend gave it to her, we saw her."

"Comes to the same thing, doesn't it?"

Did it? I was not sure. My head was confused. I only knew that I wanted to forget about Fraulein Berg for a while and would have been happy to hear that she had moved to a

different school.   But she was still with us, walking with
bowed head through the corridors, rapping on her attaché
case with red knuckles for order which she never got.   The
three of us she ignored, totally.   She did not ask any of us to
read in class, or translate.   We tried to make a joke of it and
dubbed ourselves 'The Invisibles' but we really found it
disturbing.

Harriet's parents had, of course, been livid.   She told me
that they would never have let her go away with Mrs MacCabe
if they had had any idea she was going to get up to *all that*.

"But everybody smuggles from Dublin," I objected.   "You
told me so yourself.   You told me your mother brought
through a gold bracelet the last time they went, and a silk
dress."

That was different, said Harriet.   Well, they hadn't been
taken into huts and searched, had they?   That was what had
been so ghastly about our trip, and that was what they were
objecting to.   They *might* have been searched, I pointed out,
it was only luck that they were not.

"Nonsense!" said Harriet, unable to argue any further.

The upshot of it all was that she was forbidden to associate
any more with Sally MacCabe.   The Lintons said they did not
consider her or her family to be suitable companions for their
daughter.   In school they could do nothing to prevent the
association and we three continued to sit beside one another
in class and huddle together at break-times; but walking up
the street was out, for Mrs Linton took to collecting Harriet
in the car after school every day.

"I'm sorry, Sally, really I am," said Harriet.   And I believe
that she was.

"It's all right," said Sally, trying to make out that she
didn't mind but she did.

Mrs MacCabe soon recovered from her ordeal.   A good
night's sleep and she was back to normal and able to see the
funny side.   The Night We Got Searched at the Customs

became a big joke in the MacCabe household.

I should have reckoned with Mrs Linton telling my mother but had not.

"You didn't tell me you were searched at the Customs," my mother said to me one evening when we were sitting by the fire. She was putting up a hem and I was doing my German homework. My finger slipped and my fountain pen released a blot of ink on my book. "Mrs Linton was in this afternoon," she added.

She had heard nothing about Fraulein Berg, only about Mrs MacCabe and her sister losing their clothes. I expected my mother to be livid too but, unexpectedly, there was a little smile on her lips. She shook her head.

"Millie MacCabe! Trust her!"

"You don't mind then?"

At once she grew serious. "Oh, I wouldn't say that. Well, I mean I do and I don't."

I didn't quite follow her. Did she think it was all right to smuggle or not? I asked. Of course she didn't! she answered emphatically; it *was* illegal, after all. But she went on to say that nobody was perfect, times were hard when there was a war on and people often resorted to doing things they might not do in peacetime.

"I suppose what I'm trying to say is that there's no strict dividing line between black and white, good and bad. It isn't the end of the world as Mrs Linton seems to think it is. The trouble with her is she's got no sense of humour."

I could follow her now for she was saying just what I'd often felt: that good and evil were kind of mixed up and the choice between them was not as straightforward as Miss Thistlethwaite seemed to think, or at least implied to us that it was.

I took a corner of my blotting paper and soaked up the worst of the blue blob. It went all squidgy and ended up looking a bit like a misshapen spider. My mother commented that I'd made rather a mess. I said it was only my German homework.

"Only? Don't you like German then?"

"Not much. I think I'll stop it at the end of the year. We can if we want to."

"Are you sure you want to give it up?"

"Positive," I said.

On the sixth of June, contingents of British and American forces landed in Normandy.

"This'll be the turn of the tide, you mark my words," said Mr MacCabe. "Now we'll have the Gerries on the run. A week or two and it'll all be over."

It was the turning of the tide, he was right on that, but the fighting went on for a long time, right into the following year. By the time our last week of term arrived the Allies were still struggling in Northern France.

On the second last day Harriet came into school looking very quiet. In the morning Sally and I yattered on in our usual style, exhilarated by the prospect of no more school for eight full weeks, and let her be.

At lunch-time I said, "What's up with you? Not feeling well?"

"I'm leaving," she said.

"*Leaving?*" we cried.

"Tomorrow."

Her parents were sending her to a different school on the other side of town. No doubt they considered it to be better. It was more select, her mother told my mother when she came for a fitting, and suggested that I should try for a scholarship so that I could go too but my mother told her we were quite satisfied, thank you, and saw no need for a change.

So after that we saw less of Harriet, inevitably. "It needn't make much difference," she said as we walked up the hill for the last time. "We can still be best friends."

We swore that we would and believed it. During the summer Harriet was away a lot, either at Portstewart or visiting this aunt or that uncle who lived in the country and had a stableful of horses; Sally and I went for runs on our bicycles down the coast to Cultra and Helen's Bay and one day were allowed to take the train to Bangor on our own.

The day before the new term started Harriet came to see us. "I hate the thought of that new school," she said miserably. We had never seen her look so hang-dog. Her shoulders slumped uncharacteristically. "I wish I was going back with you tomorrow."

She was dejected for the first week or two; she sought us out after school and at week-ends and told us how horrible the girls were and how utterly ghastly the teachers. Even worse than ours. We found that difficult to believe. And then she made new friends.

When we met at the shops we always stopped to talk and now we heard how nice the girls were at her new school, such super fun, and how interesting and understanding the teachers were. Not like our crabby old lot! And the school was beautiful, not like our scabby old worm-eaten dump. It was not *that* bad, we muttered, and they *were* painting some of the rooms. Not before time, said Harriet, and she hoped they were replacing the cracked windows too for the draughts were something frightful in winter, weren't they? Then she had to fly to meet Penelope or Evadne who lived in castles and dressed like princesses and were admired by every male in the city over the age of twelve.

144

For the first week in the autumn term we had Fraulein Berg for geography. Our old geography teacher had become even more decrepit during the course of the summer and been forced to give up. Miss Thistlethwaite was scraping around for a replacement but whilst she did, Fraulein Berg must hold the fort.

"Have any of you been to France, girls?" she asked.

No one had. How could we when France had been occupied for the last four years? And before the war not all that many people travelled on the continent, not in the way they do nowadays.

"Paris is a beautiful city. I am so happy that it has now been liberated and people can stroll freely again along the boulevards and sit at the pavement cafés watching the world go by." She gazed out of the window with a far-away smile as if she was there herself.

For once she had silence in her room, and our attention. We stared at her. We knew that Paris had been liberated on the twenty-fifth of August but we hadn't expected her to be pleased about that.

"Whose side is she on after all?" Sally and I asked one another uneasily as we walked up the hill afterwards. It didn't seem to be her own side, the Germans. In that case she would be a traitor, wouldn't she? "I don't know," said Sally. We despised traitors, people like William Joyce (known as Lord Haw-Haw because of his accent) who broadcast for the Germans. He was actually Irish, and not British, but he was labelled a traitor. We loved heroes, hated the weak and the treacherous. Loyalty to one's country must come before anything!

We had a very confused idea of the whole war, the way it started — no one at school had ever attempted to explain it to us — and as far as we were concerned Germany had invaded countries that were our allies in Europe and we had had to go in and save them. So it should have been straightforward: us against them.

"But what would you do if you had a horrible man like Hitler as your leader?" I asked.

"I don't know," said Sally again, wearily, and we let the subject of Fraulein Berg drop. Since that disastrous half-term week-end we had done our best not to think about her at all and had managed fairly well.

In the middle of that term she left our school. She went, we presumed, to yet another one. For the few weeks before she left, her classes had got more and more chaotic. The noise could be heard in the corridor and the adjoining rooms. We would listen to the racket, our own teacher would shake her head and then, all of a sudden, silence would fall. Miss Thistlethwaite would have arrived. Poor Fraulein Berg! She was totally unsuited to teaching but I suppose had no other way of earning her living. She left the flat over the shoemaker's shop too. Whenever I looked up I saw a woman with blond hair moving about.

Fraulein Berg dropped from our sights and minds. Harriet did not, but the gap between us widened until, looking back, we could hardly believe that we had ever been 'thick as thieves'.

On the eighth of May, 1945, we celebrated V.E. day. Victory in Europe! The moment we had been waiting for — when the war would be over — had arrived, more or less. There was still Japan to be defeated of course but it was so far away we didn't take it too much into account and, anyway, we felt confident now that the Allies would soon sort them out too. Now the lights could go on again, we would have real bananas to eat instead of mocked up turnip with banana essence, and Belfast would be like Dublin.

"I wouldn't expect too much to happen too quickly," cautioned my mother. "There'll be shortages for a long time to come."

But at least we could put away our blackout curtains. We

walked about the street late at night saying, "Isn't it fantastic? You'd think it was the middle of the day."

We went down to the City Hall to join in the celebrations. The whole area surrounding it was packed with men, women, children, soldiers, sailors, airmen. Tinker, tailor, soldier, spy... No, there wouldn't be any of them around today. There was nothing left for them to do any more.

We milled about letting the crowd take us this way and that. At times it felt like being wafted by the waves of the sea. Stay together, our mothers had warned us, so we did, hands clasped tight. We sang and danced; we cheered and laughed. The red, white and blue of numerous Union Jacks rippled high overhead. People climbed lamp posts. Soldiers chased and caught shrieking girls but although the girls shrieked they did not try to pull away. Everyone was happy. Everyone smiled. A whole new world was opening up and nothing was ever going to be the same again. Everything was going to be better.

"I can still hardly believe it," said Sally, as we travelled home, tired and scuffed, on the bus. Six years, for us, had been a long time. For anyone.

"Just imagine if you'd been living during the Hundred Years War," I said.

"Don't suppose you could have thought about war all the time though, do you?"

Even we had not thought about it every moment of the past six years.

The MacCabes had a celebration to which they invited all the branches of their family, my mother and me, and some of the boys' friends. The whole of the downstairs floor was filled so that the young ones had to sit in the porch. All the doors and windows were wide open and remained that way till long after midnight. Noise and light streamed into the garden and front street.

"There'll be no Gerries around the night to see, will

there?" said Mrs MacCabe.

She had cooked a side of beef and a leg of pork and a mountain of golden roast potatoes. She had had to do the pork in Auntie Nell's oven as there hadn't been enough room in her own. And all the ladies had been busy baking cakes and making trifles and jellies. The men were drinking the King's health and that of the boys in blue and khaki and telling one another that they could hang up their tin hats now.

"I must say I'll miss the A.R.P. post though," said Auntie Nell.

After the meal one of the MacCabe boys cranked up the gramophone and put on a record. "There'll be bluebirds over the white cliffs of Dover, *Tonight* just you wait and see," we sang.

"What about a wee dance?" cried Mrs MacCabe, kicking off her high heels.

The sitting room was cleared and the grown-ups danced there whilst we young ones took to the back garden. Mr MacCabe had to dig up most of the lawn afterwards and re-sow it. He grumbled loudly but his wife told him it wasn't every day the war ended. That was a fact he could not dispute so he went on digging and scattered his seeds and by the time small spikes of green began to push their way up he had bought a new, grander house and had this one up for sale on the market. The MacCabes moved but Sally and I remained close friends. But whenever I passed their old house, dead quiet now and respectable with never a bit of clutter visible anywhere, I always felt a little tug of sadness.

A few years later, when we were in the Sixth Form, Fraulein Berg's name cropped up again.

I was walking up the hill on my own — Sally had gone downtown to meet her boyfriend, Danny Forbes, who used to be sweet on Harriet — when old High Doh appeared at my elbow puffing and pushing his bike. The chain had broken. I commiserated.

"It's getting a bit over the hill. Like me."

I smiled in a way that I hoped would suggest that I didn't believe it, although I did.

"Oh, by the way — you remember Fraulein Berg, don't you, Kathleen?" I nodded, felt my face grow hot. "I had a letter from her this morning."

"A letter?"

"Yes. We've always kept in touch, on and off. She went to Israel, you know?"

"*Israel*?" I repeated, dolt-like.

"Yes. Seems to like it."

"That's good." I still felt stupified, unable to take in what he was saying.

"She had a terrible time in Germany of course, lost all her family in the gas chambers, mother, father, two sisters, a brother —" He broke off, shook his head. His voice was kind of choked. "You can hardly credit people would do such things, would you? She was lucky to escape. A Quaker organisation helped her —"

I could not take another second.

"I must go, Mr McGuffie, I've got to deliver a message for my mother." I felt I must be speaking wildly. He was looking at me as if I was.

I ran across the road causing a car to swerve and honk its horn at me. I turned down a side road. As soon as I knew that Mr McGuffie could no longer see me I stopped. I needed to take a deep breath to quell the nausea rising up my throat.

Fraulein Berg was Jewish! It was so obvious when one thought about it but it had not even crossed our minds that she might be. How extraordinary! We had been used to dividing up people into Protestants and Catholics in our minds but, somehow, Jews had never figured. I don't think I ever had a Jewish girl in my class, at least not to my knowledge. And of course we were young when we had pursued Fraulein Berg — when we had *persecuted* her — but even so. . .

149

"We didn't think," I said aloud, and remembered my mother saying that not thinking could sometimes be a crime.

EPILOGUE

I swallowed the remains of my coffee and made a face. It was cold.

"Wasn't that amazing?" said Sally. "To see her after all these years?"

"You recognised her?"

"Straightaway. It was her eyes. . . She didn't know me of course, not until I said who I was. She was on holiday with her husband."

"She got married?"

We had imagined her to be middle-aged when she came to teach us but Sally said she looked about sixty now so she must have been in her late twenties then.

"She had two children, a boy and a girl. She showed me their photographs. Oh, they're grown-up and married now of course."

As we were. Sally had married the owner of a bacon curing factory and they lived in Dublin with their six children. He was a Catholic. Mr MacCabe took it very badly. He saw it as a betrayal to himself and his beliefs, and would not go to the wedding. Even before he died he was not fully reconciled. Mrs MacCabe hadn't liked the match much herself, had said things like it being best to stick to your own kind, but when the first child came along she was there rocking him in her arms and saying wasn't he the sweetest wee baby you'd ever set your eyes on? But we didn't speak of all that now.

"Did you discuss that stupid business . . . of us spying on her?"

Sally laughed. "Yes, we did! And she laughed. Well, it *was* a long time ago. She said she had been a bit hurt at the time, naturally, but had realised we were just silly little girls. We had got fantasy mixed up with reality. And we *had* been subjected to a great deal of propaganda. We had been told to hate the Germans, and so we had, regardless. Anyway, after what she'd been through it scarcely touched her."

No, I didn't suppose it had. Though it had touched me. I had always wished I had got her address from Mr McGuffie and written to her but then I was not sure that I would have known what to write. But at least she had had another chance in life and been happy. I was grateful for that.

We went on to talk about Harriet, briefly. We exchanged cards with her at Christmas and sometimes received news of her through someone else. She had not got to Hollywood of course. None of us had. She had married a lawyer, a junior partner in her father's firm, and they lived in comfort on the outskirts of Belfast. Throughout the troubled times of the seventies she had managed to continue playing golf and bridge. And she had grown plump and matronly. She bore no resemblance now to Betty Grable or Ginger Rogers. If we were to meet in the street we would have difficulty passing five minutes in conversation.

"Hey, I must fly!" said Sally, looking at her watch. "I said I'd meet Kieron at four. Why don't you come over and visit us sometime, Kate? We'd love to have you. And you like Dublin, don't you?"

Indeed I did and yes, I would come, I promised. I knew I had promised before but this time I really did mean it.

Sally flew and I ordered another cup of coffee and sat on for a bit thinking of old times and our ex-German teacher. Then I rose, paid my bill and left.

At long last the file on Fraulein Berg could be closed.